Charmseekers

Books 10 – 13

Amy Tree

Illustrated by Gwen Millward

Orion
Children's Books

First published in Great Britain in 2011
by Orion Children's Books
a division of the Orion Publishing Group Ltd
Orion House
5 Upper St Martin's Lane
London WC2H 9EA

An Hachette UK Company

1 3 5 7 9 8 6 4 2

Text copyright © Amy Tree
Moonlight and Mermaids 2009
The Mirror of Deception 2009
Zorgan and the Gorsemen 2009
The Last Portal 2009
Illustrations copyright © Gwen Millward
Moonlight and Mermaids 2009
The Mirror of Deception 2009
Zorgan and the Gorsemen 2009
The Last Portal 2009

The right of Amy Tree and Gwen Millward to be identified as
the author and illustrator of this work has been asserted.

The Orion Publishing Group's policy is to use papers that are natural,
renewable and recyclable products and made from wood grown in sustainable
forests. The logging and manufacturing processes are expected to conform
to the environmental regulations of the country of origin.

A catalogue record for this book is available from the British Library.

ISBN 978 1 4440 0235 5

Printed and bound in the UK by
CPI Mackays, Chatham ME5 8TD

www.orionbooks.co.uk
www.charmseekers.co.uk

CONTENTS

The Thirteen Charms of Karisma

When Charm became queen of Karisma, the wise and beautiful Silversmith made her a precious gift. It was a bracelet. On it were fastened thirteen silver amulets, which the Silversmith called 'charms', in honour of the new queen.

It was part of Karisma law. Whenever there was a new ruler the Silversmith made a special gift, to help them care for the world they had inherited. And this time it was a bracelet. She told Queen Charm it was magical because the charms held the power to control the forces of nature and keep everything in balance. She must take the greatest care of them. As long as she, and she alone, had possession of the charms all would be well.

And so it was, until the bracelet was stolen by a spider, and fell into the hands of Zorgan, the magician. Then there was chaos!

Moonlight and Mermaids

In fond memory of Selina Young –
free spirit, sadly missed

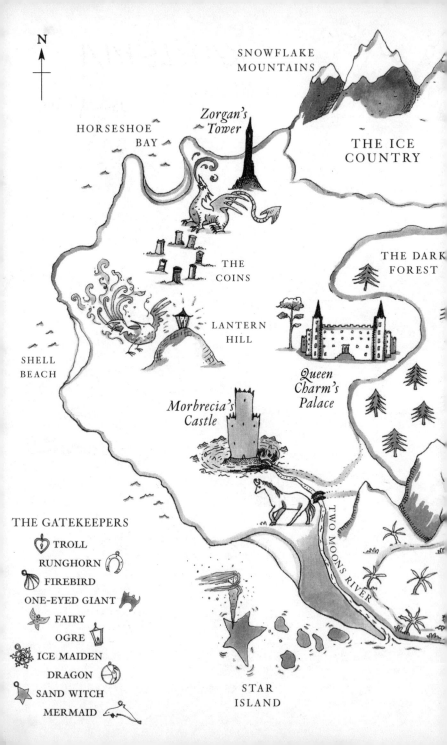

KARISMA

CAPE CAT

CLOVER FIELDS

HEARTMOOR

DOLPHIN BAY

OUNT
RTUNA

The Silver Pool

KEY
POINT

SWAMPS

JUNGLE

MERMAID
ROCK

BUTTERFLY BAY

One

A wall of water rose from the sea and came thundering towards Sesame. She clung tight to her pony's mane as they galloped along the shore – Silver's flying hooves kicking up the sand. Chasing them was Princess Morbrecia astride a giant crab! The crab scuttled sideways at an alarming speed, gaining on Sesame fast. When Sesame dared to look back, she saw Morbrecia's hair, a tangled mass of seaweed, streaming behind her in the wind. Suddenly Morbrecia's skinny arm shot out to snatch Sesame's locket and . . .

Sesame woke.

"NO!" she screamed. "No! Go away!"

Nic Brown came bursting into her room to see what was the matter. He looked puzzled as his daughter sat up in bed, shaking her head.

"What's up, Ses?" he asked. "I heard you shouting. Thought you'd been attacked by aliens!"

16

"Er, no, Dad," said Sesame. She felt silly. "I had a crazy dream, that's all. I was riding Silver and there was this massive wave and . . . oh, it doesn't matter—"

Her voice trailed off. How could she explain about Morbrecia and the crab and everything she'd seen on Star Island✱ a while ago? She hadn't told him, or her gran, Lossy, about *any* of her adventures in magical Karisma and her quest to find the thirteen silver charms. No one knew, except her special friends Maddy, Gemma and Liz, who'd been there too. They were all Charmseekers and their club was top secret!

Sesame hated keeping secrets from her dad, but she knew he'd never believe her. Who would?! He'd think she was bonkers, or just making it up. One day she *would* try to explain everything – but not yet.

Nic smiled at her reassuringly.

"You were riding Silver yesterday, weren't you? And today we're going to Water Wonderland, with a super wave machine and slides. I heard you chatting about it, before you went to bed. I reckon it all got muddled up in your dream."

* *
✱ Do you remember what happened there? You can read about Sesame's adventure in Book Nine: *Star Island*

17

Sesame nodded. It was true she *had* been looking forward to going to Water Wonderland for ages.

"I can't wait to go, Dad," she said.

✳ ✳ ✳

While Nic was making breakfast, Sesame quickly washed, dressed and bundled her swimming things into a kit bag. She was longing to wear the fab new stripy swimsuit her gran had bought her.

Sesame was halfway through the door, when she saw her necklace on the bedside table – a silver chain and locket, with tiny pictures of her parents inside – the one Morbrecia had tried to snatch (and *almost* got away with) the last time Sesame was in Karisma. That was how the clasp came to be broken but, since then, it had been repaired. She went back for her locket, put it on and ran downstairs. She found her dad in the kitchen, on the phone.

"Uh-huh . . . right . . . sorry to hear that, Mrs Green. Yes, I'll tell Sesame.

Hope Gemma will be okay. Thanks for letting me know. Bye."

"What's happened?" asked Sesame, dumping her kit bag on the floor.

"Gemma can't come today," said Nic, replacing the handset. "She's sprained her ankle playing football with her brother."

"Oh no!" wailed Sesame. "Poor Gemma."

Seconds later, her mobile jingled.

I SO WANTED 2 CUM 2DAY. MEGA MIZZ. ☹ HAVE FUN WITH MADDY + LIZ. LUV GEMMA x

Sesame replied straightaway:

WE WILL MISS U LOADS. TELL U ABOUT WW L8R. HOPE UR BETTER SOON. ☺ LOL SESAME x

Lossy arrived after breakfast. She was going to help look after the girls. Nic had been booked to take photographs at the opening of the new leisure park; he hoped to get some good pictures of Sesame and her friends trying out the waterslides and other rides. Sesame had arranged to meet her best friend, Maddy Webb, and Liz Robinson there, at eleven o'clock sharp.

Liz was waiting for them, but there was no sign of Maddy. After several anxious minutes, Sesame looked at her watch.

"Eleven-ten," she said. "Why is Maddy *always* late?"

"Here she comes," said Lossy. She waved to Mrs Webb, who'd just dropped her daughter off in the car. Maddy ran up to them, full of apologies.

"Sorry, Mr Brown . . . forgot my towel . . . had to go back . . . Mum mad and—"

Sesame rolled her eyes and grinned at Maddy.

"That's okay, Maddy," said Nic. "Glad you could make it!"

Once inside, Lossy took the girls off to a changing room. The girls chatted excitedly, admiring each other's swimsuits. Maddy wore a spotty tankini top with sea-green shorts; Liz looked great in coral pink and Sesame's stripy swimsuit fitted perfectly.

Sesame was about to leave her watch and necklace in a locker, when she read a warning notice:

The management regrets it cannot accept responsibility for the loss or theft of personal property. Please keep valuables with you at all times!

So she decided to keep them on.

Lossy and the girls met up again with Nic, at the Mermaid Café. He'd been enjoying a tropical fruit smoothie while he was waiting for them.

"Where would you like to start?" he asked. "The Rocky Creek raft ride looks fun."

"Yesssss!" chorused the girls at once.

"Too scary for me," said Lossy. "I'll settle for a Pineapple Surprise and wait for you here."

Sesame, Maddy and Liz shrieked with delight as they were buffeted about in a raft, crashing and splashing down a fast and furious creek, while Nic took action-packed pictures.

Next, they jumped over waves in the Dolphin Lagoon, and dashed through Thunder Valley Falls. Finally, they joined the queue waiting to go on The Crazy Octopus.

"For experienced swimmers only," Liz read from a safety sign. She added half-jokingly, "I'm glad I've got my life-saving certificate!"

They heard screams coming from one white-knuckle waterslide and Maddy felt her knees go wobbly.

"Mm," she said. "You might have to rescue me!"

"You'll be okay," said Sesame. "We'll race each other to the pool."

"I'll wait and see who wins," said Nic. "I should get some good pictures. Good luck!"

The girls climbed a flight of steps, then each sat at the entrance to a chute. From there the slides looked terrifying — long, twisty tubes, snaking to the pool far below.

Sesame suddenly felt her necklace tingle, sending a prickling sensation down her spine. She had the weirdest feeling something magical, something extraordinary, was about to happen. No time to think. Behind her was a queue of people waiting their turns on the slides. She looked at Maddy and Liz.

Two

The Silversmith wanders through the woods on Mount Fortuna. It is a beautiful moonlit night in the mede* of Carm, at the beginning of summer.

* *
Mede – month

She breathes deeply and enjoys the fresh smell of the pine forest; and as she walks, she thinks about recent events. News of Sesame has reached her in various ways: whispers, rumours, urchin and fairy gossip.

"I knew the moment Sesame was parted from her locket," she murmurs. "I felt the wrench of losing contact with my Seeker. It *mustn't* happen again. If only I could find a way to protect her from Zorgan, the magician—" She stops. Listens. She has heard the faintest flutter of wings. Is it a bird, or perhaps a moon moth?

It is neither. To the Silversmith's delight, she glimpses a fairy flitting through the trees – her green, gossamer gown, shimmering in the moonlight. When the fairy settles on the path in front of her, the Silversmith sees the delicate features of a girl. She smiles sweetly at the Silversmith and greets her:

"Fairnight,* Metalcharmer. I am Quilla."

* *

*Fairnight – a typical greeting, after moonrise

The Silversmith is amused to be called Metalcharmer, which she knows is the fairy name for a silversmith. Fairies believe silversmiths can charm metal, and have the greatest respect for their skills.

"Fairnight, Quilla," replies the Silversmith. "I'm pleased we meet at last."

"You fear for your Seeker from the Outworld,"* says Quilla. It is not a question.

"Yes," says the Silversmith. She is not surprised that Quilla knows what she has been thinking. "Sesame Brown is in grave danger. Zorgan is determined to put a curse on Sesame, to make her bring him the charms. For such powerful sorcery to work, he must hold something precious that belongs to her. He has been trying to steal her locket."

Quilla sighs.

"I'm afraid the magician will succeed," she says. "As you know I live backwards. I have seen the future. Zorgan *will* take possession of Sesame's locket. It is only a matter of time!"

Later, when the Silversmith returns to her workshop, her thoughts are in a whirl. She paces the floor, thinking. Thinking!

"Is there no way I can prevent Sesame losing her locket?" she says. "I know Sesame would never willingly give Zorgan the charms, but if she falls under his spell . . . oh, the consequences are too terrible to imagine! That balam* magician will empower Charm's bracelet with Dark Magic. Morbrecia will wear it and become queen, but it is Zorgan who will be in control. *He* will rule Karisma. No! I can't let this happen. There must be *something* I can do . . ."

* *
Balam — cursed or damned

29

Three

WHOOOOOOSH!

Sesame flew along the red chute – flat on her back, feet first. All the way down she had the strangest feeling she was floating on air, the wind whistling past her ears. Maddy was on the blue slide, Liz on the green. The girls were flipped this way and that as they whizzed around the twisty waterslides, until they shot into the pool –

It's like a bubble bath, thought Sesame, swimming underwater. But when she opened her eyes, she noticed something strange about the bubbles – they were going the wrong way. She knew bubbles in fizzy drinks travelled up, but these were definitely going down – and they were pulling her with them!

She looked around for Maddy and Liz; they seemed to be turning somersaults in slow motion and, when she tried calling them, no sound came out. Next thing she knew they were all tumbling, like clothes in a washing machine, faster and faster – down, down, down in a swirl of bubbles – on their way to Karisma!

POP! POP! POP!

The girls surfaced by a big rock in the sea, bathed in silvery moonlight. The water felt cold, so they quickly clambered out onto the rocky ledge. Which is when they noticed the mermaid.

"Wow!" exclaimed Maddy.

"A real mermaid!" said Liz, shaking drops of seawater off her glasses.

They stared at her in wonder. She was sitting in a magnificent oyster shell, her rainbow-coloured tail

swept elegantly to one side; around her neck she wore strings of fine pearls and entwined in her long, fair hair were the brightest red moon poppies. * She was playing a scallop-shell harp and singing:

Beneath two brightly shining moons,
Dolphins dance to mermaids' tunes.
While far below the foaming waves,
Merfolk stir, in coral caves.
Whispering tales about the sea,
Moonshine magic and mystery!

The mermaid saw the girls and waved.

"Fairnight, Charmseekers," she said. "Welcome back to Karisma. I'm Selena, Gatekeeper Ten. This is Mermaid Rock."

"Hi," said Sesame.

"I'm Maddy," said Maddy, "and this is Liz and—"

"Sesame Brown," said Selena. "Yes, we gatekeepers know all about you. Queen Charm told us you're looking for her missing charms." Selena paused. Sesame's necklace had caught her eye.

* *
* Moon poppy — a type of sea flower, found only in waters around Karisma

Mermaids love jewellery. "Ah, this is the locket I've heard so much about."

"Er, yes," said Sesame.

She looked slightly puzzled, so Selena explained:

"My friend Ramora the sand witch whispered a message in the waves. It arrived a while ago on the evening tide. It's a pretty locket. May I see inside?"

"Of course," said Sesame, opening it to show Selena the pictures of her parents. "My mum Poppy died in a car accident, when I was a baby."

It was Selena's turn to look puzzled.

"Car?"

Liz did her best to describe one.

"It has wheels and seats and doors and a motor and you . . . drive it around," she finished flatly. She could tell Selena hadn't a clue what she was talking about.

"Whatever it is," said Selena, "I'm very sorry to hear about your mother, Sesame."

"Thanks," said Sesame, firmly closing her locket with a *snap!* "When Mum died, my dad gave me her special jewellery box. It's where I'm keeping the charms." Then thinking Selena might get the wrong idea, she hastily added: "Of course, I'll be returning them to the queen when we've found them all!"

"Four are still missing," said Maddy.

"I think I can remember what they are," said Liz. "The moon, the lucky cloverleaf, the dolphin and the . . . key."

"Sesame Brown will track them down!" said Sesame.

"Well, I hope you find them soon," said the gatekeeper. "Ever since the queen's bracelet was stolen, I've noticed changes. The wind has been blowing the wrong way and the sea has got colder. All is not well for us merfolk."

35

"I think the sea is colder because the ice is melting in the Ice Country," explained Sesame. "You see, the charms help control the forces of nature. Things won't get better till they're all back together again. And I won't give up till I've found them! I wonder which one we'll find this time."

She glanced at the brightly shining moons. Perhaps they'd find the crescent moon. Selena knew what Sesame was thinking.

"Look below the waves," she advised. "You may find the *dolphin* there."

"Oh," said Sesame. "I love dolphins! They're SO playful. I saw this brill programme on TV once and—"

She broke off. Liz was looking worried.

"Um, how do we breathe underwater?" Liz asked Selena.

"Yeah," said Maddy. "Big problem."

"Follow the seahorse," said Selena. "He will help you."

"Thanks," said Sesame. "What time do we have to be back?"

"Sunrise," said Selena.

Sesame looked at her watch. The digital display had magically changed to Karisma time. It had happened before, and now the dial looked like this:

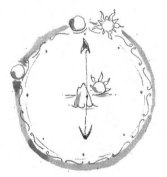

"I'm glad my watch is waterproof!" she said.

And they dived into the chilly sea.

The bandrall,* Vanda, had seen and heard everything. Selena saw her take off from Mermaid Rock, soar into the sky and fly north, towards Zorgan's Tower. She knew it was a bad sign. It sent a shiver down her tail.

* *
*Bandrall — rare flying mammal, native to Karisma

Four

From his Star Room, Zorgan searched the starry heavens, waiting for the return of Vanda. He'd sent her to spy out the land. While he waited, he marvelled at the moons.

"They are at their brightest and best at this time of year," he murmured. "A magical sight! No doubt the Moon Spirits are celebrating tonight . . ."

His thoughts were suddenly interrupted by the sound of leathery wings, beating at the window. It was Vanda. Zorgan let her in and she perched on a chair, while he fed her choice morsels of toad liver and worms.

"Anything to report?" he asked.

Vanda snapped greedily at a wriggling worm. It dangled from her beak, before slithering down her gullet.

"Mermaid Rock," she croaked. "Sesame Brown and two others. Seeking under the sea."

"Spallah!"* exclaimed Zorgan, delighted the Charmseekers were back. "Was Sesame wearing her locket?"

Vanda gobbled a titbit of toad, then replied:

"Pictures inside."

"What pictures?" snapped Zorgan.

"Parents," said Vanda. "Poppy."

"Ah!" said Zorgan. "Better than I thought. You have done well."

For a while the magician was deep in thought. He paced the floor of his Star Room, fiddling with a gold medallion. Before long, the corners of his lips curled into a cruel smile.

"I have an idea," he said.

* *

*Spallah — excellent. A triumphant expression

Zorgan summoned Nix and Dina to his library, where he kept his magnificent collection of spell books. The pixie girls were by his side in an instant, their sharp crystal eyes glinting in anticipation, eager to carry out their master's wishes.

"You will go to Mermaid Rock and find Sesame Brown," said Zorgan. "I'm giving you one last chance to bring me her locket. If you fail, I'll turn you into fishpaste!"

"Yes, Master!" they chorused, shuddering at the venom in his voice. It was true, their previous attempts to steal Sesame's locket *had* failed, but they were determined to succeed this time. If they didn't, they knew Zorgan would carry out his threat. Nix and Dina whirred their wings, in readiness to take off, but Zorgan held up his hand.

"Stop! I haven't finished. For this mission I'll be making a slight alteration to your appearance. A temporary disguise to fool Sesame and assist you in your task . . ."

The pixies were programmed to obey Zorgan without question. Nevertheless, they couldn't help wondering what he had in store for them.

Apprehensively, they watched as he opened his spell book (at a page he'd previously marked) and twitched his magic wand. Flashing lights and fizzing sparks flew from the wand as he pointed at each pixie and intoned:

"With steely wings and fishy tail,
A mermaid you shall be.
Make haste and dare not think to fail –
I must curse S-e-s-a-m-e!"

The spell worked straightaway and took the pixies by surprise. Their legs changed into scaly fish tails and they felt most peculiar. Besides, they couldn't stand up.

"Woooah!"

cried Nix, falling flat on her face.

"Whoops!"

shrieked Dina, wobbling about. She flipped and flapped her tail, trying to get her balance.

Zorgan wasn't amused. "Doofers!"* he yelled. "Flap your wings. You're *flying* mermaids! Get going and don't come back without the locket."

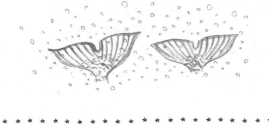

* *
✻ **Doofer** – idiot of the first order. Brainless

43

The Silversmith, meanwhile, has been thinking about her Seeker. She glances at the thirteen magic candles — four remain burning brightly for their charms yet to be found. She crosses her workshop to stand by the window. The silvery moons bathe her in pools of light as she recalls her chance meeting with Quilla.

"If Quilla is right, if Zorgan steals Sesame's locket I must thwart his plans. I *am* a metalcharmer. I made the magical charm bracelet. I have mystic powers over all things silver. . ."

She closes her eyes. Soon she is in a dreamlike state, and into her dreams drift the gentle Moon Spirits. They take the Silversmith by the hand and fly with her to Mermaid Rock, whispering the whereabouts of Sesame — and a magical charm, waiting to be found.

The Moon Spirits cast their shimmering beams below the waves. Now the Silversmith sees her Seeker, glimpses her silver locket . . . and, in her trance, she softly murmurs:

Gentle moonbeams shining bright,
Cast your magic spell tonight!"

In the blink of an eye, she is awake. The Moon Spirits have gone, but memories of all she has seen and heard in her dream remain.

"The Moon Spirits will help Sesame tonight," she says. "I don't know how, but they will."

Five

Sesame, Maddy and Liz found the seahorse waiting for them.

"Follow me," he said. "I'll take you to the Mer Elder."

The pearly-pink seahorse with its tube-like nose, spiny body and curly tail led the girls down through freezing, green waters to the seabed. They passed a mother dolphin and her calf playing with a piece of seaweed, 'talking' to each other in clicks and whistles.

Sesame was amazed to discover she could understand their language.

"They're playing seaweed tag!" she told Maddy and Liz.

Maddy was just wondering how much longer she could hold her breath, when the seahorse stopped at a grotto. Moonbeams shone through crystal windows, so the girls could see everything clearly. As they looked around, their eyes opened wide in astonishment. The walls and roof were decorated with exquisite mosaics, made from thousands of tiny shells, pearls and precious stones – pictures of sea-dragons, mermaids, dolphins and whales; brightly-coloured coral and strange-looking fish.

In the middle of the grotto stood a white marble fountain, which was spouting bubbles. Some mermaids were having a game with one bubble, big as beach ball, flicking it about with their tails.

"I wish we had tails," said Liz. "It looks fun."

The others nodded.

"Bubbleball," said the seahorse. "It's a favourite game down here. It helps to keep them warm. If they didn't, their tails would turn blue with cold! Now come and meet the Mer Elder."

47

The Mer Elder was sitting on a clamshell; he wore
a gold ring in one ear and had spiky orange hair.

"I'm sure he can help you," said the seahorse.

"I hope so," said Maddy. "I'm gasping for some
air!"

"Welcome, Charmseekers," said the Mer Elder.
"If it's air you need, come with me."

He swam to the fountain and scooped up some bubbles.

"Long lasting air bubbles," said the Mer Elder. "Swallow these and you'll breath like fish." He blew the bubbles at them and said some magic words:

"GILL INFLATIMUS AORTA!"

After taking deep breaths, Sesame, Maddy and Liz felt much better.

By now the girls were surrounded by inquisitive merfolk. They'd heard about the famous Charmseekers and wanted to see what they looked like! One mermaid, who'd been playing bubbleball, came forward.

"I'm Meranda," she said.

"Hi," said Sesame, and she introduced the others.

"Pretty beads," said Maddy, admiring the glass necklace Meranda was wearing. "It's like the one I found on Star Island."

"I bought it from the urchins," said Meranda. "They make jewellery and ornaments from things they find on the beach. Urchin craft is very popular with mermaids."

"We know them," said Sesame. "It's great they're recycling their left-behindings."

"What *are* you talking about?" said Liz, who hadn't met the urchins.

"Tell you later," Sesame promised. "We *must* look for the charm."

"May I come?" asked Meranda. "I know the sea like the back of my tail."

The girls thought it was a great idea, so they showed her their Charmseekers secret hand sign.

"Now I'm a Charmseeker, too!" said Meranda proudly.

"Setfair,"* said the Mer Elder. "I hope you find all the charms soon, Sesame. If the sea gets much colder, we shall perish!"

"The charm could be anywhere," groaned Maddy.

Liz peered through her glasses at the vast expanse of sea.

"Mm," she agreed, "and we haven't much time to find it."

Sesame snatched a look at her watch.

"Yes," she said. "Karisma time is weird. The nights are shorter than ours. We must hurry." She turned to Meranda. "Where do you think we should start?"

"Dolphin Bay," suggested Meranda. "But if you haven't much time, the quickest way there is through a spooky kelp forest."

* *
* Setfair — goodbye and good luck

51

"Dolphin Bay sounds good," said Sesame. "Don't worry. If we keep together, we'll be okay."

So, with a flick of her tail, Meranda headed for Dolphin Bay. Sesame, Maddy and Liz were good swimmers; they could keep up with the mermaid quite easily. As they were rounding Key Point, Sesame was aware of sounds travelling through the water. She thought they sounded like the clicks and whistles she'd heard earlier – only these were different. The high-pitch tone of the signals told her something was wrong.

"Wait!" she cried. "That sounds like a dolphin. I think it's in trouble."

"I can't hear anything," said Maddy.

Liz strained her ears.

"Nope. Not a thing," she said.

"Sesame's right," said Meranda. "They're coming from the other side of the forest. Follow me!"

As soon as they entered the gloomy place, the Charmseekers felt a sense of foreboding. Meranda was right. The kelp forest *was* spooky! The giant seaweed towered tall as trees, their fronds waving in the murky water. Nothing grew here except kelp, and everywhere was eerily silent.

53

Sesame did her best to keep close to Meranda's tail, but the further they went, the gloomier it became, until *bump* – she swam headlong into a kelp stalk. It was slimy, and thick as a tree trunk.

Yuk!" she cried, pushing herself away with such

force she accidentally turned a somersault. When Sesame tried to right herself, she realised she'd lost all sense of direction. Help! she thought. Which *is* the right way up? Worse still, she couldn't see Maddy, Liz or Meranda anywhere.

To her dismay, she was completely alone.

Six

Sesame shivered. It was icy cold and dark in the kelp forest. Even the moons couldn't shine their light here. Every so often the silence was broken by squeals of distress, which Sesame knew were coming from a dolphin. She took deep breaths to calm the panicky feeling welling up inside her tummy.

"Don't panic," she said. "Chill out! Think, Sesame. Think! If Sesame Brown can track charms down, finding Maddy, Liz and Meranda shouldn't be a problem. Right? Follow the signals and we *should* all meet up with the dolphins."

Sesame brushed aside trailing seaweed fronds which were grabbing at her hair, and began swimming towards the squeals. It wasn't long before she noticed two shadowy shapes moving below, and then her imagination ran wild. Oh, no! she thought. Girl-eating sharks! Her heart was pounding. She'd never felt so frightened. She was sure she'd be eaten alive. Suddenly Sesame came to a clearing, where moonbeams reached even these dark waters. Now she was relieved to see the shapes weren't sharks, they were mermaids!

Sesame's locket had started to tingle and goose pimples were running up and down her spine. Was it a good sign or a warning, she wondered, turning to face the oncoming mermaids. Perhaps Meranda had sent her friends to help. Yes, that was it!

But as the mermaids closed in, Sesame's locket tingled again and again and, just in time, she saw the glint of a steely wing in the shadowy moonlight . . .

She gasped in horror.

"You're not mermaids," she said. "You're Nix and Dina in disguise!"

"And *you're* in trouble!" said Nix gleefully.

56

"Give me your locket NOW," said Dina. "Or else."

The menacing pixie lunged at Sesame. She was quick, but Sesame was quicker. She jinxed behind a rock then, dodging both pixies, darted between the kelp like a fish.

By now, Sesame's eyesight had adjusted to the gloomy light and she swam scarily fast through the forest. Nix and Dina, finding it difficult to control their tails, kept getting tangled in seaweed! Although Sesame wasn't aware of it, she did have another advantage over the pixies; the dolphin had picked up Sesame's sound vibrations through the water, and was guiding her with *clicks* to Dolphin Bay. Nix and Dina heard them too, but they didn't know what they meant. Soon Sesame had left Nix and Dina behind – but they were determined to catch her up.

Through the Scary Kelp Forest

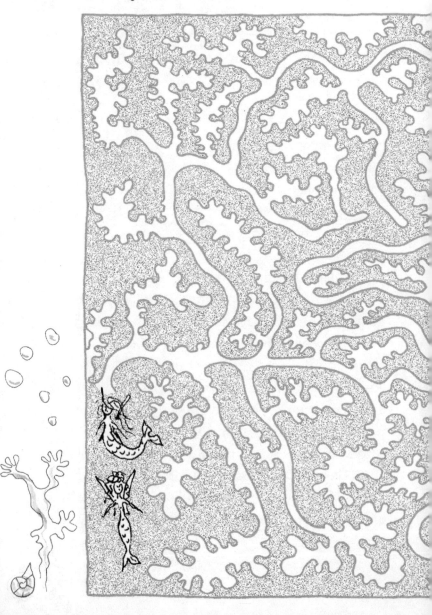

The pixies must catch Sesame and steal her locket. Can you see the path Nix and Dina must take to find her?

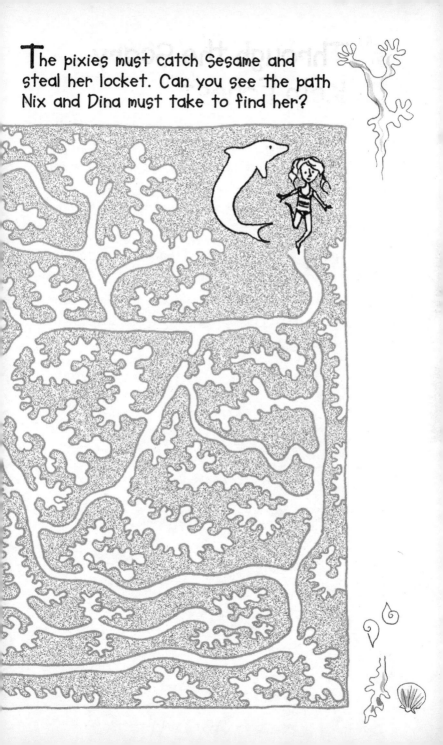

Sesame found the dolphin stranded on the seabed, tangled in fishing net. Nearby her calf was swimming in circles, whistling in distress.

"Oh, you poor thing!" cried Sesame, reaching through the net to stroke the dolphin's nose. "You must be exhausted. And you've injured your flippers."

Her thoughts raced. What could she do? She talked to herself, trying to think.

"Dolphins need air, I know that. But there's no way I can take her to the surface to breathe. Not on my own. Which reminds me, where *are* Maddy, Liz and Meranda? I SO hoped they'd be here. The dolphin must have air or she'll die!"

She looked around hoping, by some miracle, to see the others. But there was no sign of them – or, for that matter, of Nix and Dina.

"Phew!" she said. "At least I don't have to worry about the pixies!"

As she spoke, bubbles came popping out of her mouth – and *that* gave Sesame an idea . . .

"Magic bubbles!" she cried. "I'll give some of mine to the dolphin."

Sesame located the blowhole at the top of the dolphin's head, then she gently blew bubbles inside. To her delight it worked. The mother was out of immediate danger, and her calf flipped a somersault for joy. But she was still caught in the net.

"I'll soon have you out of there," Sesame promised.

However, untangling the net proved more difficult than Sesame imagined; it was tightly wound round her tail and flippers. While Sesame was struggling with it, she got her foot caught and then her arm got stuck. Twisting and kicking, she struggled to free herself, but it was no good.

She was snared
too! And just when she
thought things couldn't get
any worse – they suddenly did.
Nix and Dina finally caught up with her.

"Got you!" shrieked Nix, her eyes glinting with malicious pleasure. Her victim was wrapped like a parcel.

"Just where we want you," added Dina. "You don't stand a chance, Sesame Brown!" She made a grab for Sesame's locket.

"NO!" screamed Sesame. "Go away!"

Echoes of her nightmare rang in her head. Only this time her dad wasn't there to comfort her. This was for real! Sesame gripped Dina's wrist with her free hand. The pixie was pulling at her locket and Sesame could feel the chain cutting into her neck.

Now Nix was at her throat –
tugging, tugging, tugging at the
locket, until *SNAP!* The clasp broke.

"GOT IT!" cried Nix triumphantly,
holding Sesame's locket aloft.

"Our master shall have it at last!" said
Dina.

"NO!" wailed Sesame. "Give it back!
PLEASE!"

And none of them saw the monstrous octopus
swiftly heading their way . . .

Seven

In another part of the forest, Maddy, Liz and Meranda had been searching for Sesame. For a while Meranda had followed the dolphin's signals but when they'd stopped, she'd lost her way.

"I'm sorry," she said. "It all looks strange."

"Never mind," said Liz. "I'm sure we'll find Sesame soon."

"If Ses doesn't find us first," said Maddy, trying to sound cheerful.

At last, they found a way out of the horrid forest and into Dolphin Bay. Bright moonbeams filtered through blue-green waters and shed their light on a coral reef. As they swam over it, Maddy and Liz saw shoals of strange-looking fish; and, clinging to the reef were purple sponges, pink anemones and delicate white sea-fans.

"Wow!" exclaimed Maddy. "It's like a tropical garden."

Liz noticed a clump of gorgeous bright red flowers.

"What are those?" she asked Meranda.

"Moon poppies," said the mermaid. "They only open their petals in the moonlight."

When Maddy looked again she saw something small, something *silver*, caught in the petals and glistening in the moonlight. She gasped.

"It's the dolphin charm!"

The others peered at it too.

"Oh!" sighed Meranda. "It's beautiful!"

"I *wish* Sesame was here," said Liz.

65

Maddy was reaching for the charm, when Meranda shouted a warning.

"Look out! Puffcap!"*

An enormous jellyfish topped with a blobby poison cap was hovering overhead, waving its tentacles. The girls backed away terrified.

"It looks like an alien!" said Liz.

"Puffcaps are

very

dangerous," said Meranda. "Moon poppies are their favourite food. They'll sting anything that gets in their way!"

Maddy glanced first at the charm then at the jellyfish, which was about to land on the poppy.

* *

*Puffcap – a large jellyfish, so called because its poison sack looks like a cap

66

"That puff-thing's going to eat it!" cried Maddy. "We can't risk losing the charm."

"R-i-g-h-t," said Liz, dodging a deadly tentacle. She'd been stung by a jellyfish once, and remembered how much it had hurt.

Thoughts whirled inside Maddy's head. What would Sesame do? I bet she wouldn't give up. Well, I'm a Charmseeker too! I've made up my mind . . .

"I'm going for the charm," she announced fearlessly.

"*Please* be careful, Maddy," Meranda pleaded. "Puffcaps can kill!"

Liz could tell Maddy was determined to rescue the charm, and tried to reassure her.

"You'll be okay," she said. "I've done my life-savers badge. I know how to rescue a casualty—"

"Er, yeah, thanks, Liz," Maddy cut in. "Let's hope I won't need your life-saving skills!"

They gave each other their secret hand sign for luck, then Maddy took a deep breath.

"Here goes!"

Everything happened quickly. As Maddy plucked the charm from the poppy, the puffcap shot out a stinging tentacle, whipping it around her wrist.

"Aaaaaaaargh!"

shrieked Maddy, dropping the charm.

It felt as if she'd being stung by a million wasps at once! Her head was spinning. She saw stars. She felt dizzy . . . then she couldn't remember a thing.

In a daze, Meranda watched the dolphin charm spiral slowly down, until it disappeared through a crack in the rock. Liz's eyes were fixed on Maddy, hanging in the water, limp and lifeless.

"I'm coming," she yelled. She took Maddy firmly by one arm and supported her chin, then with Meranda close behind, she towed her to the surface.

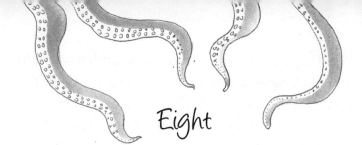

Eight

Meanwhile Sesame had been experiencing some hair-raising events of her own.

Trapped in the net with the dolphin, she could only stare wide-eyed at the giant octopus. Nix and Dina, who had their backs to the monster, mistook Sesame's petrified look for shock – they thought she was upset at losing her locket. But they soon realised their mistake. Swiftly, stealthily, the octopus came from behind and squirted them with smelly black ink! The pixies got the surprise of their lives.

"UGH!"

spluttered Nix, choking on the foul-tasting fluid.

"YUK!"

yelled Dina, swallowing a mouthful of ink.

69

In the confusion, Nix let go of the locket. Sesame saw it falling through the water. She pushed her free arm through the net, reaching, stretching as far as she could, in a desperate attempt to catch hold of it. For one exhilarating moment, she felt the chain brush the tips of her fingers – then it floated away.

As the inky water cleared, the pixies' laser-sharp eyes spotted the falling locket. Tears of frustration ran down Sesame's cheeks as she watched Nix and Dina dive for it. But the octopus was ready for them. His writhing tentacle seized Dina by her hair and flung her aside; he coiled another round Nix's tail and shook her like a rag doll.

"Ouch, ow, ow!" yelled Dina.

"Help! Stop!" cried Nix.

Suddenly, despite everything, Sesame giggled and whispered to the dolphins:

"I think the octopus is on our side!"

Nevertheless, the ruthless pixies hadn't forgotten their master's fish paste threat. Wrenching herself free, Dina snatched up the locket; then with a swish of their tails, the pixies swam off as fast as they could go.

Sesame was filled with dismay all over again – nothing could stop Zorgan casting his spell now!

Sesame was right about the octopus. He *was* friendly!

"I came straightaway when I heard the distress calls," he told her. "When I saw those pixies I tried to help you, too. The merfolk said you were a Charmseeker!"

"You were brill," said Sesame.

The octopus helped Sesame from the net, then together they released the dolphin. They thanked the octopus for his help and he went home to his cave.

Sesame looked at her watch. Time was whizzing by! "It's *ages* since I saw Maddy, Liz and Meranda," she told the dolphins. "I wonder what's happened to them?"

Just then the dolphins picked up mermaid signals through the waves and Sesame knew something must be wrong.

"What's up?" she asked.

"Your friends are in trouble. Come with me!"

71

Nine

The Silversmith knew the instant Nix wrenched Sesame's locket away. A pain stabbed her chest and she saw a shadow fall across the moons.

"Hushish!"* So, Zorgan's wretched pixies have succeeded."

In her mind's eye she sees Sesame's locket, and again she implores the Moon Spirits:

*Gentle moonbeams shining bright
Cast your magic spell tonight!"*

Far from the clutches of the octopus, Nix and Dina leaped from the sea like flying fish. They landed *splat! smack!* on the peak of Mermaid Rock – where their tails fell off! Instantly, they were transformed into themselves.

* *

*Hushish – a word used to express dismay

"Good," said Nix, stretching her legs. "I hated that slimy fishtail!"

"Me, too," said Dina. "Now we can return to our master."

Before they took off, Dina couldn't resist holding Sesame's locket up to look at it. Her eyes sparkled with delight as she recalled the look of pain on Sesame's face. The locket shone in the moonlight . . .

Suddenly a moonbeam struck it like a bolt of lightning! Dina shielded herself from the blow; the locket sprang open — and out fell the picture of Poppy. Nix and Dina watched the tiny picture flutter away on a breeze.

"Leave it," said Nix. "We've got the locket. That's all that matters. Let's go!"

And with a whir of steely wings, the pixies flew off to Zorgan's Tower.

Selena the Gatekeeper was anxiously keeping watch for the Charmseekers' return.

"It will be sunrise soon," she said. "How strange! Tonight the moons are shining more brightly than ever."

As she spoke, a bright light struck Mermaid Rock. Selena saw a fragment of paper come spinning like a leaf – twisting and twirling, until it landed by her tail. The mermaid picked it up and gave a little gasp of surprise.

"This belongs to Sesame," she said, recognising the picture from Sesame's locket. "What can have happened?"

About this time, Sesame was being reunited with her friends. The dolphin mother and her calf had taken Sesame to Maddy, Liz and Meranda.

"Thank you," Meranda whispered to the dolphins.

Sesame was shocked when she saw Maddy – her best friend looked weak and pale. She listened while Liz described what happened. When she'd finished Meranda quickly added:

"Maddy was very lucky to survive the puffcap sting. They're deadly dangerous!"

"Oh, Maddy," said Sesame. "You were SO brave!"

"I feel a bit funny," said Maddy. "But, Ses, the dolphin charm! I dropped it—"

Her voice trailed away and she looked as if she was going to faint again. The dolphins gently held her with their flippers.

"I saw where the charm fell," said Meranda. "I'll take you there, Sesame."

Sesame looked at her watch. The sun was beginning to creep over the horizon.

"Great!" she said. "I reckon we've got about ten minutes left before sunrise. Come on. There's no time to lose!"

"I'll stay with Maddy," said Liz. "Good luck!"

Sesame dived with Meranda and followed the mermaid down to the coral reef. Moonbeams lit their way, which slightly puzzled Sesame, because it was nearly morning.

Soon they passed the patch of moon poppies Meranda and the girls had seen earlier. The mermaid looked cautiously around for the puffcap, but thankfully it was nowhere in sight. Eventually, they came to the place where the charm had disappeared.

"It went in there," said Meranda, pointing to a yawning crack in a rock.

Sesame peered in. She couldn't see a thing, until a shaft of moonlight caught a speck of silver. It twinkled like the brightest star in a black, velvet sky. Sesame's tummy flipped with excitement as she reached in . . . Her fingers closed around something small and smooth, and slowly she eased it out. It *was* the little dolphin charm! Even at this depth, the charm seemed to sparkle with a magical light of its own.

"Oh, it's fabulous," said Sesame, holding it so Meranda could see.

"It looks like a *real* dolphin," said Meranda.

Sesame clasped it in her hand, afraid she might lose it. For a split-second she thought of her locket slipping away, and she held the charm more tightly still. Can't worry about that now, thought Sesame. We must get back to the gate!

The dolphins took the Charmseekers for the ride of their lives – skimming, jumping, leaping over the foaming waves – all the way to Mermaid Rock!

Selena was at the gate.

"Hurry!" she urged the girls. "It's almost sunrise. Sesame, I have something for you." She held up a small mermaid purse. "It contains something precious."

"Thank you," said Sesame, briefly wondering what it could be. "Is there room for this, too?" She opened her palm to show Selena the dolphin charm. She thought the little purse would be the perfect place to put it.

"Of course," said Selena, opening the purse for Sesame to drop it in. "I'm delighted you found it. Well done, Charmseekers. Setfair!"

When Sesame, Maddy and Liz turned to go, there were loud cheers from Meranda, the Mer Elder and all the merfolk. A little way out to sea, the dolphins leaped for joy. The Mer Elder blew a stream of rainbow-coloured bubbles, then an enormous wave swept them off Mermaid Rock and they were plunged into a sea of sparkling, bubbling foam.

Down they went with the bubbles, past the little seahorse and the octopus, faster and faster, until –

Whooooosh! — they splashed into The Crazy Octopus pool, at Water Wonderland.

"Terrific!" said Nic. "Great action pic. You all arrived together!"

Sesame, Maddy and Liz scrambled out of the pool in a daze. The waterslides had been amazing, but nothing compared to their adventures in Karisma! And Sesame and Liz were still concerned about Maddy's jellyfish sting.

"Are you okay?" whispered Liz.

"I feel fine," said Maddy. "I think those bubbles did the trick!"

"Come on," said Nic. "Let's find Lossy. She's waiting for us at the Mermaid Café."

"Where's your locket, Sesame?" asked Lossy, as soon as they met up.

Maddy shot Sesame a look of startled surprise. It was the first time she'd noticed it was missing.

"Er, I must have lost it—" began Sesame.

"Oh, what a shame," exclaimed Lossy. "I expect you dropped it on one of the rides. Perhaps someone will find it and hand it in. You never know your luck."

Later that evening, when Sesame was alone in her room, she sat on her bed remembering some of the amazing things that had happened.

"The octopus looked SO scary," she told her teddy, Alfie. "At first I thought he was going to eat me. But he was great. I'm glad he gave those horrid pixies a hard time."

She opened her jewellery box; Queen Charm's silver bracelet and nine magical charms lay there. Sesame fished the mermaid purse from her pocket and took out the happy, playful dolphin charm.

"Look, Alfie," she whispered. "Isn't it lovely? Just like the real ones I saw today! Now there are only three more charms to find," she told him, as carefully she placed the dolphin in the box with the others.

Sesame was so pleased to have found the dolphin charm that she almost forgot what Selena had said about the purse. She remembered now: 'It contains something precious.'

She gave the purse a little shake and . . . out fell the photo of Poppy.

"Oh!" gasped Sesame, staring at the tiny image of her mother smiling back at her.

Tears trickled down her cheeks as she thought of her favourite necklace and how the pixies had taken it. Even worse, the wicked magician, Zorgan, might be holding it right now. She shuddered.

And then something dawned on her. Staring at Poppy, Sesame realised the *most* precious thing about her locket was what it contained. She treasured the little picture of her mum, and it was safe and sound. As for her dad . . . he was here, for real! Besides, she had loads more photos of him. Sesame wiped her tears. She placed the picture of Poppy inside the jewellery box with the charms – precious things together – and closed the lid. Things didn't seem so bad, after all.

Ten

Three magic candles remain burning for their charms yet to be found — the silver crescent moon, the cloverleaf and the key. A tell-tale wisp of smoke curls from the candle that bears the dolphin's name, and the Silversmith claps her hands with delight. She knows it safe with Sesame, in the Outworld.

Seated at her dressing table, she brushes her fine, silvery hair and thinks about the day she knows will soon come, when all the charms are found, and the magical bracelet will be returned to Queen Charm.

"Three more charms to find and Sesame will have completed her quest," she says. "Nothing, no *nothing* must stand in her way . . ."

As she speaks, the red sun rises and a ray of fiery sunshine strikes the mirror glass. For a split-second she is dazzled by the light; she rubs her eyes and looks again and now she sees the terrifying vision of Zorgan! The magician is scowling and from a finger he dangles a locket. It belongs to Sesame, of course, and the locket is open. The Silversmith peers more closely. The place where Poppy's picture should be is quite empty!

"Ah," she sighs, as the vision fades. "The Moon Spirits have worked their magic. All is not lost!"

But she knows her Seeker will be tested – it will take all Sesame's courage and strength to defeat Zorgan's tricks and treachery . . . but that is another story, it must be told another day!

The
Mirror of
Deception

For Charlotte and Chris — with love A.T.

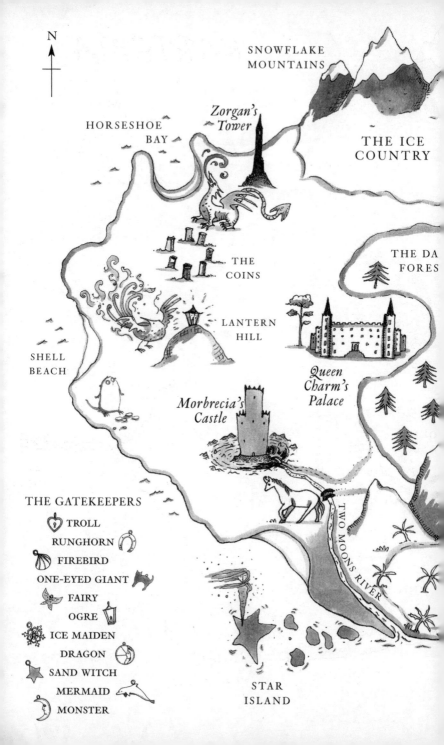

KARISMA

CAPE CAT

CLOVER FIELDS

HEARTMOOR

DOLPHIN BAY

OUNT
RTUNA

The Silver Pool

KEY
POINT

SWAMPS

JUNGLE

MERMAID
ROCK

BUTTERFLY BAY

One

One morning, not long after Sesame's last visit to Karisma, Queen Charm invited her good friend, the Silversmith, to the palace.

"I've received a puzzling letter from one of my gatekeepers," said Charm, handing the Silversmith a parchment scroll.

Your Majesty,

I am pleased to inform you that the Charmseekers, Sesame Brown and Maddy Webb, have found your dolphin charm!

Unfortunately, while Sesame was here, Zorgan's pixies snatched her locket and flew away with it. I regret there was nothing I could do to stop them. I fear Sesame may now be in some kind of danger from the magician in the Tower!

Your faithful servant,

Selena

Gatekeeper Ten,
Mermaid Rock

"I'm delighted Sesame has found my silver dolphin," said Charm. "It's wonderful news! But what's this about Zorgan and a locket?"

The Silversmith sighed.

"Your Majesty, I confess I've known about Zorgan's attempts to steal Sesame's locket for some time. But I didn't want to worry you. You've *quite* enough to think about! Once or twice I've used my mystic powers to prevent his pixies stealing it. Unfortunately this time I couldn't stop them."

"What's so special about it?" asked Charm.

"It's Sesame's favourite," said the Silversmith. "It matters to her a great deal. In possession of such a precious belonging Zorgan could . . ." She paused, knowing that what she was about to say would come as a shock. "Zorgan could enchant Sesame to make her bring him your bracelet!"

"Quisto!" ✱ exclaimed Charm. "This is terrible! Isn't there *something* we can do?"

The Silversmith tried to calm her friend.

"I believe the locket is not *quite* so useful now to Zorgan as it might be. He appeared to me in a vision.

* *
✱ Quisto – an exclamation of surprise

93

I saw him holding Sesame's locket. It was open. One of the pictures she keeps in it was missing. He looked furious."

Charm gave her a quizzical look; wondering whether she would *ever* understand her mysterious friend.

"What do you mean?" she asked.

"There's a chance the enchantment will fail," said the Silversmith. "But Zorgan won't give up easily. He'll have other tricks up his sleeve!"

A look of grim determination clouded Charm's delicate features.

"I've been patient too long," she said. "The future of Karisma is threatened by this slitey ✷ magician.

He must be defeated! I'll call a Kluster* today. Please come. I should value your good advice."

⁎

Later that day, a group of important palace officials gathered round an enormous table in the State Room, discussing what to do about Zorgan. Seated on one side of Charm was the Silversmith, and on the other was her most trusted guard, Officer Dork.

There, too, was the Chancellor, a stout man called Robustus. He puffed out his cheeks and banged his fist on the table.

"Zorgan is a menace!" he stormed.

* *
*Kluster – a meeting of important officials

95

"I agree," said the Prime Minister, a quietly spoken man with bright red hair and a beard. "The vermy* magician is indeed a menace. The cause of all our troubles."

"We need a plan," murmured the Head of the Planning Department. He had spent most of the meeting doodling on a pad with his quill pen. He had underlined the word 'PLAN' several times.

Officer Dork cleared his throat.

"Er, we could call out the army, Your Majesty," he suggested. "Finish Zorgan off, once and for all!"

The beautiful young queen looked from one to another, twisting a strand of fair hair round her finger.

"Surely we can stop him without resorting to violence," she said. "Things are bad enough without making them worse! The next time Sesame comes to Karisma, we must protect her. The sooner she finds all the charms and returns them to me, the better. Zorgan is powerful, but he's no match against my magical charm bracelet."

* *
* **Vermy** — miserable worm

96

"Yes," said the Silversmith. "Let's try to resolve this peacefully. But if all else fails, we may *have* to take Zorgan by force!

Two

Princess Morbrecia entered Zorgan's Tower and threw back the hood of her black, velvet cloak. The princess had covered herself from head to toe, so no one could recognise her. It would never do for the sister of Queen Charm to be seen visiting the wicked magician!

As Morbrecia climbed the one hundred and ninety-five twisty steps to the Star Room, she recalled her last visit to the tower, many medes * ago. She remembered that night as if it were yesterday . . .

* * * * * * * *
* Mede – month

I brought the bracelet to Zorgan, just as we'd planned. I risked everything, but I did it. He promised to empower it with Dark Magic and make me queen. But he ruined everything when he threw the charms away.

"I'll never forgive him, the magwort!" ✱ Morbrecia spat the last word. At the top of the stairs she paused to catch her breath, before opening the heavy wooden door to the Star Room. Stepping inside, her mood of displeasure quickly changed to delight.

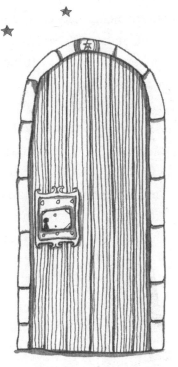

✱ **Magwort** – probably the worst name you could call anyone! General term for a fool

Since childhood Morbrecia had been fascinated by sorcery. It thrilled her to see the weird and wonderful things Zorgan used to make magic. Suspended from the ceiling was an amazing clockwork universe, with moons and planets whirling around the sun. Bottles of slime-green potions, fizzing, frothing and fit to explode, jostled for space on a shelf next to jars of jellied frogs, snakes' eyes and worms. Leather-bound spell books, a flickering black candle, one skull and a wand lay piled haphazardly on a table. Near a window stood Zorgan's telescope and, on a plinth, was his glowing crystal ball. Vanda, the magician's pet bandrall,* was perched on a chair. She eyed Morbrecia suspiciously.

Zorgan greeted Morbrecia with the thinnest of smiles.

"Welcome, Your Highness," he said, bowing.

* * * * * * * * * * * * * * * * *
*Bandrall – rare flying mammal, native to Karisma

100

Morbrecia wasn't fooled by Zorgan's gesture of respect. She'd learned to be wary of the sly magician. But she wanted the bracelet more than anything and she needed his help to get it. Besides, only Zorgan could empower the charms with Dark Magic, which was *so* much more dangerous and exciting than white magic. She'd have fun causing havoc and mayhem! Her eye caught something silver, glistening in Zorgan's hand and she wondered if he'd found a missing charm.

"What's that?" she asked.

Zorgan showed her the necklace nestled on his palm.

"Sesame's locket!" exclaimed Morbrecia, recognising it at once. She'd tried to steal it herself on more than one occasion. "We have it at last. Quick! Put a curse on that interfering Outworlder." *

Zorgan frowned. He opened the locket and showed Morbrecia the empty space where there had once been two little photographs. Nic Brown smiled out at them, but Poppy Brown's picture was missing.

"Where is it?" asked Morbrecia.

* *
* Outworld – the name Karismans call our world

"My foolish pixies lost it at Mermaid Rock,"* said Zorgan. He glared at Nix and Dina, who were quivering in a corner. "I have severely punished them for their mistake. They were lucky I didn't turn them into fish paste! But what's done is done. I believe the gatekeeper found the picture and returned it to Sesame—"

"So?" snapped Morbrecia. "You still have the locket. What are we waiting for? Cast the spell!"

Morbrecia could barely contain her excitement as Zorgan prepared to perform the curse. From the toppling pile of spell books he selected a dusty tome:

Curses Ancient and Modern.

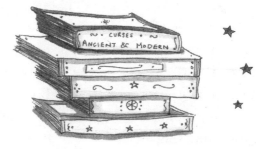

* *

*Mermaid Rock – do you remember what happened? You can read about Sesame's exciting adventure in Book Ten: *Moonlight and Mermaids*

He blew the dust from its cover, then tapped it with his wand and commanded:

"Open! Page two hundred and eighty-four."

As if by magic, the book opened at the right place. Zorgan held up Sesame's locket, gazed into his crystal ball and chanted:

"Oh, crystal ball reveal to me
The whereabouts of Sesame.
My spell shall make the Seeker see,
She must bring all the charms
to ME!"

Three

Sesame couldn't believe it. She had just come third in the Pole Bending event, riding Silver in her very first gymkhana.

"Well done, Ses!" said Nic Brown, as he walked over to the horsebox with his daughter. "I got a great photo of you racing over the finish line."

"Thanks, Dad," said Sesame, smiling happily. She gave Silver a pat; a bright yellow rosette was fluttering from his bridle.

Sesame's riding instructor, Jodie Luck, was there too. She beamed at Sesame.

"You were brilliant," she said. "You've worked so hard. Keep it up. You're my star pupil!"

When they reached the horsebox, Sesame got Silver ready for the journey back to Jodie's yard. She was putting on his travel rug, when she caught sight of Olivia Pike on her dappled-grey mare, Misty Morning. Olivia went to Sesame's school and kept her pony at Jodie's too. Sesame thought Olivia was a spoilt brat, because she never stopped bragging about owning her own pony. They were *not* the best of friends!

Olivia had won several events at the gymkhana and was smugly showing off her red rosettes. Sesame groaned as Olivia made a point of riding slowly by.

"Better luck next time, Sesame," she called out. "Bet you wish you could ride as well as me. *And* had a super pony like mine!"

"Silver is the best pony in the world," retorted Sesame hotly. "So there!"

Jodie heard and came over to calm things down. Olivia ambled off smirking, leaving Sesame fuming.

"I *know* I should have ignored her," she admitted to Jodie. "But Olivia is SO annoying!"

"Time to go, I think," said Jodie tactfully. "It's been a super day. Don't let *anyone* spoil it! Believe in yourself, Sesame. You did your best."

✳ ✳ ✳

That evening, Jodie came to supper with Nic and Sesame, and stayed to watch a DVD. Jodie had been going out with Sesame's dad for several months; Sesame had grown very fond of her and the feeling was mutual – and they shared a love of horses!

Sesame glanced at the TV. Nic had put on an old-fashioned black and white film with romantic background music.

"Dad, what *are* you watching?" she said.

"*Moonlight Madness*," said Nic. "A classic."

"Mm," said Jodie, reaching for a box of tissues. "This one always makes me cry. I love it."

Sesame rolled her eyes.

"I'm going to chill," she said. "See you two later."

She went up to her room; Chips and Pins raced ahead to lie in wait for her under the bed. When they shot out to pounce on her feet, she skipped aside laughing, then proudly pinned up the photo of her and Silver that her dad had taken at the gymkhana. She put her yellow rosette beside it.

"Perhaps one day I'll ride in the Olympics," she told her teddy, Alfie, "and win a gold medal." She giggled. "If I won gold, Olivia Pike would go green with envy!"

Next she put on a CD – her favourite band, Crystal Chix – and went online to chat to her best friend, Maddy Webb. After they'd chatted about Sesame's gymkhana win for a while, Maddy said:

MadWebbgirl@mailwizard.net says:

I've got to wash my hair 2nite. Wot RU doing?

seekerSes@zoom.com says:

Chilling out. Dad and Jodie are watching a film. Moonlight Madness. Sooooo boring!

MadWebbgirl@mailwizard.net says:

Sounds romantic! Do you think your dad and Jodie will get married?

seekerSes@zoom.com says:

I don't know. Maybe.

MadWebbgirl@mailwizard.net says:

Cool! If they did, Jodie would be your new mum!

Sesame stared at her computer screen. The words 'new mum' jumped out at her. She'd never thought of anyone taking the place of her mother before.

MadWebbgirl@mailwizard.net says:

Ses, RU OK? Sorry if I said the wrong thing.☹

seekerSes@zoom.com says:

Yes, I'm fine. Honestly.☺ Jodie's great. I just never thought of her in that way.

MadWebbgirl@mailwizard.net says:

Oh, must go. Mum says I've got to wash my hair NOW. See U at SKL 2moz. Talk 2U then. Nite nite. Sleep tite. x

seekerSes@zoom.com says:

See you. Mwah Mwah xx

Sesame shut down her computer. Maddy's comment about Jodie set her thinking. How *would* I feel about having Jodie as my mum? I'm not sure. I was a baby when Poppy died. I don't remember much about her, but I think I'd feel guilty calling Jodie 'Mum'. Anyway, Dad and Jodie aren't even engaged! It may never happen.

Going to her bedside table, she opened her special jewellery box where she kept the magical charm bracelet and charms. They sparkled in the lamplight as she opened the box. She'd also placed the little photo of her mother from her locket there for safe-keeping and, seeing Poppy Brown's happy face, she picked up the photo and looked at it closely. Then, on impulse, she tucked it into her pocket. I might not have my locket, but I can still keep this close to me, she thought.

Sesame sighed. "I love Dad," she told Alfie, "and I can tell Gran *most* things. But perhaps it would be nice to have a mum . . ."

Seeing the bracelet and charms, Sesame thoughts quickly turned to Karisma. She'd found ten charms and was anxious to find the three that were still lost. Picking up the bracelet, she admired the one charm clinging to it – the perfect little heart with a lock.

"The queen lost her bracelet *ages* ago," she told Alfie. "She must be sad. I hope I can return it soon."

Almost without thinking, Sesame began to fasten the other charms to the bracelet; one by one she added the horseshoe, shell, cat, butterfly, snowflake, lantern, coin, star and dolphin. They twinkled like stars on a frosty night.

"Oh!" she exclaimed, her eyes shining with pleasure. "It's beautiful. I wish I had one like it."

Holding the bracelet, she became aware of a tingling sensation prickling the tips of her fingers. It reminded her of the way her locket used to tingle, when something extraordinary was about to happen. That was before Zorgan's nasty pixies had snatched it, the last time she was in Karisma. Nic and Lossy thought she'd lost it swimming at Water Wonderland. She couldn't tell them what had really happened. Was the charm bracelet trying to tell her something? she wondered.

Chips and Pins were acting strangely too. They were hissing at something in Sesame's wardrobe mirror; their fur stood on end and their tails bristled like brushes.

Without warning, a dazzling light streaked across the glass, as if it had been struck by lightning. Instinctively, Sesame shielded her eyes and the cats flew under the bed.

When she dared to look again, she gasped. Reflected in the mirror was a man dressed in a long, dark robe; and from his finger he dangled her locket. Sesame knew, without the shadow of a doubt, that she was looking at Zorgan!

Four

Sesame tried to scream, but she couldn't. She shut her eyes tight, then opened them again, hoping the vision had gone. But it was still there – real as anything.

Zorgan fixed her with his cold, black eyes. Slowly, rhythmically, the magician swung the locket like a pendulum – this way, that way, to and fro – so that almost immediately Sesame became mesmerised by the swaying movement. She felt herself drawn like a magnet to the magician, and all the time she could hear his haunting, hypnotic voice coaxing her to give him the charms:

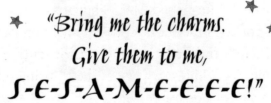

"Bring me the charms.
Give them to me,
S-E-S-A-M-E-E-E-E!"

Dimly, she saw his hand reaching out to her. She felt weak and sleepy. Oh, so sleepy! Until . . .

Suddenly stars swirled from the bracelet! Dazed and confused, Sesame snapped out of the trance. Just in time she stepped back from the mirror.

"No! No!" she yelled. "The bracelet belongs to Queen Charm. I'll never give it you. Never!"

Thoughts raced inside her head. She *must* protect the bracelet at all costs! Slowly she backed across the room, not daring to take her eyes off Zorgan for a second. She dropped the bracelet in her jewellery box, then closed the lid with a *snap!* Phew! she thought. The charms are safe, I hope!

Zorgan was furious, but managed to hide his rage. It would never do for Sesame to think she'd won.

"Blatz!"* he cursed, through gritted teeth. "The power of the bracelet has broken my hypnotic spell. But I'm not finished yet. I'll twist the truth to make Sesame see things *my* way. She'll bring me the charms of her own free will."

* *
*Blatz — a really angry exclamation

115

Zorgan smiled at the young girl who had confronted him so boldly, with arms folded and an expression of defiance on her face. He spoke quietly, his voice oozing false concern:

"Brave Sesame, you've been sadly misguided by the Silversmith. She is using you to carry out her plan. It is *her* you should fear, not me. When you've returned all the charms to the queen she will have no further use for you. She has tricked you and I fear your life is in danger."

Sesame listened, her heart thumping. She wished Maddy were here! She could hear Chips and Pins softly growling under the bed. She stood her ground. I'm not silly, she thought. Zorgan's faking.

"I don't believe you!" she shouted. "Go away!"

The image of Zorgan remained.

"Listen," he said, struggling to keep his temper under control. "The Silversmith is really a wicked witch! She's in disguise. She's cursed the charms. This notion about them controlling nature is nonsense. They're the *cause* of all the bad things happening in Karisma, and it's her doing!"

Sesame was horrified. This was the opposite of everything she'd been told. She was sure the magician must be telling lies.

116

"No way!" she said. "That's so not true."

"I'm afraid it is," said Zorgan. "The Silversmith is cunning. She befriended Queen Charm and made her the bracelet. She persuaded her it was a magical force for good. For a while all was well. But it was all part of the Silversmith's plan to cause misery and chaos."

Sesame looked puzzled.

"Why would she do that?" she challenged.

"The Silversmith wanted to create havoc," said Zorgan. "The witch has power over all things silver. She *controls* the charms! When it suited her, she intended to put her plan into action. Win the people's respect. Charm would appear weak and the witch would seize the throne."

Sesame thought Zorgan was beginning to sound convincing. Supposing he *was* telling the truth?

"What about Morbrecia?" asked Sesame. "I know she's after the charms."

"Morbrecia is the *true* queen of Karisma. She is the eldest princess," replied Zorgan. "She stole the bracelet from Charm to thwart the Silversmith. Morbrecia knew there was a chance I could break the curse, so she brought them to me.

I tried and failed. So I cast them away. The Silversmith has used YOU to get them back—"

"How?" broke in Sesame. "I've never met her."

"The witch possesses mystic powers," said Zorgan. "She controls you through this…"

Zorgan held up her locket.

"Give it back!" cried Sesame. "It was your horrid pixies who stole it."

"For your own good," said Zorgan soothingly. "I *had* to stop the Silversmith communicating with you, before it was too late. Morbrecia tried to warn you too. Don't you see? If you return the bracelet to her sister, the Silversmith will have won. Your reward will be the witch's CURSE!"

Zorgan's last words boomed in Sesame's ears like thunder. She staggered, reeling from the shock of realising that, after all this time, she might have been under the spell of a wicked witch! It was chilling.

When she looked at the mirror again, the vision of Zorgan had vanished. In its place was a swirling mass of stars, drawing her into a whirlpool of golden light. Before she knew what was happening, the looking-glass melted away and she was spinning round and round, faster and faster, through a magical golden light . . .

Once more, Sesame was on her way to Karisma.

Five

Sesame tumbled through time, spinning in the vastness of space, until she drifted down across a silvery sea, to land –

BUMP

– on a beach. She picked herself up and looked around.

"I know I'm in Karisma," she said. "But I wonder where I am?"

She half expected to be met by a gatekeeper – that's what usually happened when she arrived in Karisma – but this time she was disappointed. There was no one about. Scrambling up the shingle to the foot of a cliff, she came to a rocky cavern; the entrance was barred by an iron gate, its rusty ironwork forged into a design of ferocious beasts, which Sesame thought looked very frightening. On one side, roughly chiselled into the rock was the number eleven, and on the other, the words:

RING IF YOU DARE!

Suddenly she remembered what she'd once been told about Gatekeeper Eleven – he was a monster who ate his visitors! She gulped at the thought, then realised she had to face him. "I must go through the gate, or I might not get out again. I hope the monster isn't hungry!"

She took a deep breath and rang the bell . . .

Clang! Clang! Clang!

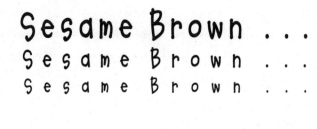

"WHO'S THERE?"

boomed a voice, so loud and fierce it made Sesame jump. She felt like making a run for it, but didn't. Instead she called out:

"Sesame Brown!" and her name reverberated round the walls.

Sesame Brown . . .
Sesame Brown . . .
Sesame Brown . . .

"WHAT DO YOU WANT?"

came the reply.

"I've c-c-come to look for the ch-charms," stammered Sesame, her knees knocking. "I'm a Charmseeker!"

There was a pause, then:

"COME IN!"

The gate swung open by itself, and Sesame stepped inside a huge cave, dimly lit by lanterns.

"Anyone there?" she called out nervously.

At the sound of shuffling feet, she turned and was astonished to see a weird-looking creature, only half her size. He had an extraordinarily large head, bulging eyes and a body covered in purplish skin, attached to which was a tail. In one hand he held a speaking-trumpet.

"Quinch," he said, extending a skinny arm

to shake Sesame by the hand. "Welcome to Karisma!"

Sesame was flabbergasted. She couldn't believe this pathetic creature had nearly frightened her to death! Quinch must have read her thoughts.

"I'm not fierce," he confessed. "I use this to scare people." He put the trumpet to his lips.

WOOOOOAAAH!

"Scary, huh?"

Sesame rolled her eyes.

"Yeah, great," she said. "Er, by the way, I've heard you . . . eat people. You call them your *elevenses.*"

Quinch squinted at her through bulbous eyes.

"Who told you that?" he said.

"The troll at Gate One," said Sesame.

Quinch laughed and slapped his sides.

"I know that troll," he said. "He likes a good joke. No, of course not. Me, eat people? Yuk! But don't tell anyone. You'll ruin my reputation!"

124

Just then his tummy rumbled loudly.

"All this talk of food has made me hungry," he said. "Time for buttered beans. Would you like some?"

"No, thank you," said Sesame politely. She thought she'd wasted enough time already. "I must look for the charms. The moon, the clover leaf and the key are still missing. Sesame Brown will track them down!"

Quinch led the way up a flight of stone steps, which zigzagged crazily inside the cliff. When they reached the top, they stepped out into warm, mid-morning sunshine.

"Phew!" said Sesame, slightly out of breath. "Where are we?"

"Shell Beach," said Quinch, indicating the beach where Sesame had landed far below. She could see some familiar places too: Lantern Hill, Charm's Palace, Morbrecia's Castle . . . and, away in the distance, a soaring column of black rock. Zorgan's Tower! Although it was daytime, Sesame was fascinated to see two crescent moons shining brightly above the tower. The way the moons were positioned in the sky reminded her of the Charmseekers' secret hand sign! She was sure it was a clue, and quickly showed Quinch what she meant.

"Perhaps I'll find the *moon* charm at Zorgan's Tower!" she told the gatekeeper.

Quinch looked horrified.

"No one goes there," he said.

"Well, I have to," said Sesame firmly. "What time does the gate close?"

"Listen for the bell," said Quinch. "You must return before it strikes eleven. Setfair!* And watch out for the magician!"

* *

* Setfair – goodbye and good luck

127

Six

Meanwhile, in his Star Room, Zorgan had spotted Sesame through his powerful telescope. He'd failed to hypnotise her, but he was determined to think of some other way to persuade her to bring him the charms. And Morbrecia was impatient for results.

"Your stupid spell didn't work!" complained the princess, who'd been with him all the while. "What now?"

"Smoke and mirrors," murmured the magician, ideas whirling inside his head. "Shades and shadows cloud her eyes . . . a feathered friend . . . a maze of lies!"

"What *are* you talking about?" snapped Morbrecia.

"Listen," said Zorgan. "Here's what we'll do . . ."

On this particular morning, in the eleventh mede of Kaleg, the Silversmith is thinking about Sesame too. She is walking on Mount Fortuna and notices the two moons above Zorgan's Tower. She knows it is the time of year when the moons shine especially bright, but something about their appearance gives her cause for concern. Weeks have passed since the Kluster at the palace, at which Charm had given orders for plans to be drawn up to take Zorgan by force, if need be. Officer Dork and his men were to protect Sesame when she returned, but as yet there has been no sign of her. The Silversmith has spent many anxious days waiting for her Seeker to return, but she knows it's not something she can hurry. Seeing the moons strangely positioned over the tower, she wonders if this is a sign. I fear Sesame may soon be in danger, she thinks.

Quickly she runs down the mountainside and enters her workshop. Straightaway her gaze falls upon the thirteen magic candles; three burn steadfastly for their missing charms.

"I'll do what I can to protect Sesame," she whispers to the candles. "Only three more charms to find. She *must* finish her quest. I can't let Zorgan win!"

She lights a tinder-stick of mystica* and before

long, the air is filled with its fragrant aroma. It calms her, as she prepares to use her mystic powers.

Seating herself at a small elegant table, she places her fingertips lightly on its surface and closes her eyes. Soon she's in a trance and fleeting images from the past, present and future flit through her head like moths in the moonlight . . .

"I see the bracelet," she murmurs. "The power of the charms defeated the magician. Good! Ah, my Seeker is here. I see her with a bird. I see . . . a *magic mirror*! What is Zorgan's plan? He will stop at nothing."

* *
*Mystica – an aromatic plant, native to Karisma. The petals produce a sweet smell when burned

The vision fades and the Silversmith opens her eyes.

"There's no time to lose. I must call upon the Moon Spirits. I know they will help, if they can."

✻ ✻ ✻

Sesame set off along the cliffs, heading north, following a path by the sea. It was summer and the sun felt hot on her back as she walked along, deep in thought. She was thinking about the vision of Zorgan in her wardrobe mirror; he'd said some disturbing things and they came back to haunt her now . . .

"Zorgan said the Silversmith is really a wicked witch. She cursed the charms and wants to rule Karisma. If I return the bracelet to Queen Charm, I'll be helping the Silversmith to cause chaos. Is Zorgan telling the truth? Perhaps not. I know *he* wants the bracelet. And why have I never met the Silversmith? Is she hiding something? What about Queen Charm? Oh, I don't know. Zorgan says Morbrecia is the *true* queen. Is she? That would explain why he wants the bracelet, to give to her. It's very confusing!"

Sesame plunged her hands into her pockets and felt the photo of Poppy there, which was reassuring. She remembered her mother had been a journalist, investigating stories. She wondered what Poppy would make of this!

Sesame went on mulling things over, trying to make sense of it all. Once or twice, she had the uncanny feeling that Zorgan was near; she kept looking over her shoulder to see if he was there, but it seemed she was alone. Before long she came to Horseshoe Bay, where the path divided and she turned right, towards the tower. With a twinge of unease, she saw it was not far away – and again and again she sensed a supernatural presence, although she could see nothing.

The sun was hotter than ever. Her throat felt tight and dry and suddenly Sesame felt *very* thirsty. By a curious coincidence, just as she was thinking how desperate she was for some water, she came to a spring, bubbling from a rock. She cupped her hands beneath the flow and drank – gulping mouthfuls of crystal clear water.

"Brill!" she exclaimed, wiping the drips from her chin with the back of her hand.

As she did so, she was startled by the *swish* of wings. For a split-second, a shadowy shape blotted out the sun and, glancing up, Sesame gave a little cry.

Perched on the rock and watching her every move was a huge, black crow.

Sesame recovered quickly. It was only a bird, and the spring water had refreshed her. She felt much better. She thought the crow looked magnificent, with his shiny blue-black beak and gleaming feathers. She was delighted when he spoke.

"Feeling better?" said the crow, cocking his head at the spring. "Cool water on a hot day. Nothing better! Where are you going?"

Sesame pointed to the tower.

"I'm looking for the lost charms," she told him. "I think I'll find the moon charm there."

"Ah," said the crow, sharp eyes glinting. "I hope you find it. You must allow me to show you the way."

"Thanks!" said Sesame. "Have you met the magician? There's loads I'd like to know about him."

"I know Zorgan well," said the crow, a crafty smile turning the corners of his beak. "We shall talk as we go along."

133

So the two set off.

Since drinking the water, Sesame had been feeling a *little* light-headed. "Probably too much sun," she said to herself, and she thought no more of it. Soon, she was happily chatting to her companion, telling the crow all about the Charmseekers and her quest to find the charms.

For his part, the crow spoke favourably about Zorgan and, with every step of the way, Sesame grew more and more convinced the magician might be someone she could trust. But as they approached the tower, Sesame noticed a chill in the air and shivered. The sun wasn't shining any more and nothing grew in these parts – not even a blade of grass. Sesame thought Zorgan's Tower looked spooky in the moonlight as they walked in its long, dark shadow and soon they were standing at the magician's door.

Seven

The tower rose from the bleak landscape like a serpent ready to strike. Above it hung the crescent moons, like a Charmseekers' sign in the sky.

Goosebumps prickled Sesame's skin. Despite the crow's reassurances about Zorgan, she couldn't help feeling a bit afraid now that she was there. Close up, the tower *did* look scary! Turning to the crow, she was dismayed to find she was alone. The crow had disappeared. He had simply vanished into thin air.

"Okay," Sesame told herself. "Don't be silly. Hurry up and look for the charm!"

She decided to start at the door and search around the base of the tower.

But when she looked, the door wasn't there! In its place was a shimmering mirror, giving off an eerie, green glow. She went and stood right in front of the mirror, expecting to see her own image reflected in the glass, but instead she saw twinkling fairy lights and could hear the sound of music and laughter. As she reached to touch the mirror, to see if it was real, the glass melted – and she stepped through a magical mist. In the distance she heard the bell strike six.

Clang!

Clang!

Clang! Clang!

Clang! Clang! Clang!

To Sesame's surprise, waiting for her on the other side of the mirror, was Morbrecia. She smiled and took Sesame gently by the hand.

"Don't be afraid," said Morbrecia. "I'm going to show you what happened a long time ago. Maybe then you'll see how the Silversmith has tricked you. Believe me, you're in great danger!"

Sesame couldn't believe her ears. Surely this wasn't the scheming princess she'd come up against before? *This* Morbrecia was friendly!

"R-i-g-h-t," said Sesame. "Where are we going?"

"To a party," said Morbrecia. "Follow me!"

It all began at Charm's seventh birthday party. I was nine. I'm two years older than my sister. We were so excited because Zorgan the Court Magician was giving a Magic Show. But that day something happened to spoil everything!

A fairy called Quilla came to see my parents, King Orin and Queen Amilla.

The Silversmith sent her, to tell them a silly story about me. Quilla said my name began with the letter 'M' and it was a BAD omen! 'M' upside-down turns into 'W' and stands for Wicked Witch! So she told my parents I should never become queen. Charm must wear the crown, not ME! And they believed Quilla. When Zorgan told me, I was very upset. It wasn't fair. I'm the eldest.

I should be queen of Karisma!

Hm!
I can see why
Morbrecia is so
angry.

The party scene faded into a foggy haze. When it cleared, Sesame was standing by a deep pool full of silver. She stared at the vision in awe.

The Silversmith gave the bracelet to my sister at her coronation. She told her the charms controlled the forces of nature. It was rubbish. They were CURSED!

On the eve of Charm's coronation, the Silversmith took the charm bracelet and dipped it three times in the Silver Pool. Then she invoked the spirit of Agapogo the dragon, to breath fire on it to seal the curse. Against her will, Agapogo was forced to obey the witch. But the dragon vowed one day she would seek revenge.

I'm afraid Charm was fooled by the Silversmith. She was taken in by her mystic mumblings! But I tell you, Sesame, the Silversmith means you harm. Once you've returned the charms, you'll be of no further use to her. She will be rid of you!

Oh dear! It looks like the Silversmith *is* a witch!

The image wavered, then faded in a misty cloud. Sesame blinked and the scene changed again. This time she was in Zorgan's Star Room, on the night he threw the charms away.

I managed, only by putting myself in great danger, to take the bracelet from Charm because the Silversmith had unleashed the curse. The charms were causing misery and chaos!

It was all part of her plan. When it suited her, she was going to take control of the charms and restore order. My sister would appear weak, whereas the witch would gain everyone's respect. Before long she would have overthrown Charm and seized the throne!

Anyway, I took the bracelet to Zorgan to break the curse. He tried all kinds of spells but nothing worked. So he threw the charms from the tower to disperse their Dark Energy.

142

The charm bracelet IS beautiful.
I would love to wear it! But it's
dangerous, Sesame. In the wrong
hands, it can only do harm. You must
believe me!

Morbrecia's words echoed eerily in Sesame's head as the vision fragmented in a cascade of glistening charms. Sesame found herself back where she started – in front of the mirror, looking in. She felt a bit dizzy. She reached into her pocket for the photo of Poppy. Smiling back at her from the mirror was Zorgan and in his hand he grasped her locket!

Eight

Sesame stared at the mirror. Was the magician real, or was he just another illusion? Everything around her *seemed* real – the tower and the crescent moons above.

The peals of the gate bell sounded nine times and she knew time was slipping by fast. Zorgan sounded real enough too, when he spoke:

"Now do you understand, Sesame?" he said. He toyed for a moment with her locket. "You've seen what happened. If you want to help Karisma, you'll bring me the charms."

Sesame hesitated, thinking fast. I'm a Charmseeker! My quest is to return the magical bracelet to Queen Charm. At least, I thought it was. But maybe I've been tricked by the Silversmith? If the charms are cursed, perhaps I *should* give them to Zorgan? Oh, I wish I knew what to do! She looked at the magician patiently waiting, and knew she *had* to say something . . .

"Okay," she said slowly, pulling the photo of Poppy from her pocket. "But I want my locket. Now!"

Zorgan hissed. He held up his hand and the silver locket glistened in the moonlight. His patience with Sesame had run out and he could no longer disguise his anger.

"Do you dare try to bargain with me?" he said, in a chilling tone. "You may have your locket IF you promise on your mother's name you'll bring me the charms!"

Sesame shuddered at the venom in his voice. Holding tight to the photo she was aware of another, kinder voice echoing in her head: *Believe in yourself, Sesame. Believe in yourself.* And in that instant any thoughts she may have had about trusting Zorgan disappeared. She saw Zorgan for what he really was – a scheming, wicked magician!

"NO!" she yelled at him. **"NEVER!"**

What happened next took Zorgan completely by surprise. The locket in his hand turned scorching HOT. Without warning, the necklace shimmered with heat and burned his fingers – just as the magical charm bracelet had done, so many medes ago.

"OWWWWOOOOOOOo!"

howled Zorgan in agony.
He flung the locket from
the mirror and it landed at
Sesame's feet. Before she knew what
was happening, there was a blinding FLASH!
She saw the crescent moons, reflected in the mirror shining so brilliantly they dazzled her. The beams were the brightest, fiercest light she had ever seen!

Stronger and stronger they blazed, until suddenly the mirror itself shattered into a million slivers of broken glass!

Sesame jumped back, shielding her face from the blast. When she looked up, she saw pale, ghostly shapes dancing for joy in the moonlight. From somewhere in the tower she heard Zorgan bellowing with rage, yelling for Nix and Dina. Moments later, she stooped to pick up her locket. It felt wonderfully cool to *her* touch.

"Brill!" she said, quickly slipping the photo of Poppy back into its place and putting the locket on. "I can't believe I've got it back." As she fastened the clasp with a *click!* she felt a familiar tingling sensation at her neck — the way her necklace always tingled when something extraordinary was about to happen. Her tummy flipped. She held her breath. Looking down she caught a tell-tale glint of silver, just where her locket had been when it had fallen. Bathed in gentle moonlight, where before it had lain hidden in the long, deep shadow of Zorgan's Tower, was the magical moon charm!

Sesame picked it up, allowing herself a moment to admire the perfect little crescent moon with its smiling face, before putting it safely in her pocket. Just then she heard the distant *clang* of the gate bell — ten strikes! Panicking, she knew she'd have to run like the wind to get back before the gate closed. Would she make it in time?

Clang! Clang! Clang! Clang! Clang! Clang! Clang! Clang! Clang! Clang!

Sesame was never quite sure what happened next, or how she found herself at the gate on the very last stroke of eleven. Everything happened so quickly.

She could still hear Zorgan yelling at Nix and Dina to go after her. Glancing over her shoulder, Sesame glimpsed their steely wings glinting in the moonlight, then she was running flat out, faster than she'd ever run before, her feet barely touching the ground. It was as if she was being carried along on a magical beam of light.

Meanwhile, behind her, brilliant moonbeams criss-crossed the path to block the pixies' view.

Even their sharp eyes couldn't penetrate the beams, and they soon lost sight of Sesame. Suddenly Sesame saw the gate . . . Quinch at the bell . . . clanging, clanging . . .

"Wait!" cried Sesame.

"Hurry!" shouted Quinch.

"Nine. Ten. ELEVEN!"

Sesame fell through the gate, tumbling down and around, over and over, through haze of golden stars until . . .

BUMP!

She tumbled out of her wardrobe mirror, back into her room.

Sesame sat on the floor, her head spinning, until Chips and Pins came out from under the bed and demanded her attention. She picked up the cats and gave them a cuddle, burying her face in their fur.

"Look," she said, showing them the mirror. "It's okay. The horrid magician has gone."

Leaving the cats to play, Sesame went to her jewellery box and opened it. The bracelet was there – ten charms securely in place. Carefully she took the silver moon charm from her pocket and fastened it with the others, so that now eleven charms glistened and shimmered radiantly with a magical light of their own.

"To think Zorgan nearly tricked me into giving them to him," she said. She smiled to herself. "No chance! I'm a Charmseeker. Sesame Brown will track the charms down . . . *and* give them back to the queen!"

She put the charm bracelet in the box and closed the lid, then unclasped her necklace and put it by her bed.

"Everything's okay now," she told her teddy, smiling.

✳ ✳ ✳

Later, when Nic came up to say goodnight, he found Sesame tucked up in bed and half-asleep.

"Great film," he said. "Plenty of action. Sad ending. Jodie was in floods of tears! You okay?"

"I'm fine," she said sleepily. She yawned. She'd seen plenty of action herself this evening!

Nic caught sight of her locket on the bedside table.

"How did that get there? Did you find it in with your swimming things after all?" he said. "Where was it?"

But Sesame didn't answer. She had fallen sound asleep.

Nine

The Silversmith sighs as she looks at the thirteen magic candles. One more has flickered and gone out – it is the candle that bears the name of the crescent moon.

Now only two candles remain glowing, burning brightly until their missing charms are found.

She thinks of Sesame and feels once more a close bond with her Seeker, now that she has her locket back. She draws comfort from knowing that she played her part in thwarting Zorgan today. A little smile of satisfaction plays about her lips as she imagines how surprised he must have been to burn his fingers on the locket. And she is so proud of Sesame for seeing through his lies – he twisted the truth, but she wasn't taken in. She will see her quest through to the end, she is sure.

Only Zorgan stands in her path — Sesame has walked through his mirror of deception and defeated him this time . . . but she will have to face him again, and this time she may have to take him by force.

But that is another story. It must be told another day.

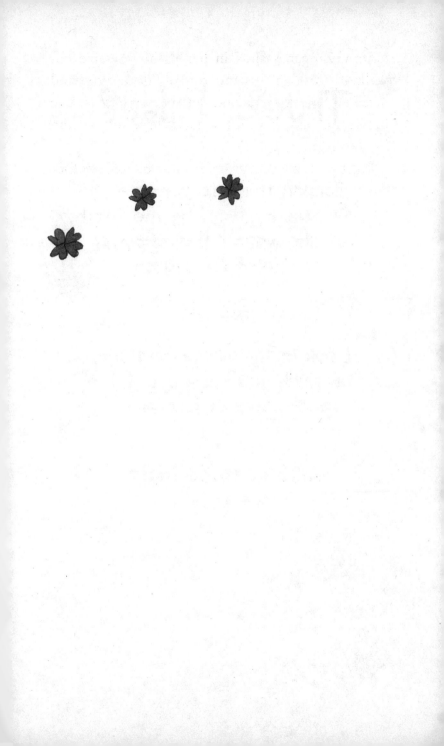

True or False?

Zorgan tried to confuse Sesame by twisting the truth, but she wasn't fooled by his tricks of deception.

Look in the mirror and see how much you know about the magical world of Karisma!

Which of these facts are true?

1. Princess Morbrecia stole the charm bracelet, because it was cursed and causing havoc.

2. The Silversmith mysteriously "communicates" with Sesame through her necklace.

3. Zorgan threw the charms away to destroy their Dark Energy.

4. Agapogo, the dragon, vowed to take revenge on the Silversmith.

5. Queen Charm is Morbrecia's younger sister.

Solution: 2 and 5 are true!

Zorgan and the Gorsemen

For Jonathan and Jenny with love — A.T.

KARISMA

CAPE CAT

CLOVER FIELDS

HEARTMOOR

DOLPHIN BAY

OUNT
RTUNA

The Silver Pool

KEY
POINT

SWAMPS

JUNGLE

MERMAID
ROCK

BUTTERFLY BAY

One

Sesame was trapped in Zorgan's Tower! The witch had slammed the door shut and turned the key. From a window, Sesame saw her sitting astride a broomstick, her tattered black rags flapping like the wings of a crow.

Sesame couldn't believe she'd been tricked so easily into parting with the magical charm bracelet. By chance, she'd met a beautiful young woman with long, silvery hair and sparkling eyes walking near Queen Charm's palace. The friendly stranger had called herself the Silversmith and promised to return the bracelet to the queen.

Sesame believed her, but as soon as she had taken hold of the bracelet, the woman changed into an ugly witch! Next thing she knew, Sesame was locked in the magician's tower, with no idea how she'd got there. She was very, very frightened.

Suddenly the witch flew to the window and Sesame stared in horror at her ghastly face, which was more wrinkled than an old potato. The hag gloated at Sesame through the glass. From a bony finger, she dangled the silver charm bracelet . . .

"Give it back!" cried Sesame. "Let me go!"

The witch cackled.

"Foolish child," she croaked. "I'll do no such thing. I've no further use for you. Soon you'll be nothing but a heap of bones, Sesame Brown! *Sesame*—"

"—Sesame, come *down*! Breakfast's ready!"

Sesame woke to hear her dad, Nic Brown, calling from downstairs. She sat up, shook her head and realised everything had been a ghastly nightmare. Her digital alarm clock was buzzing on her bedside table. It was 9:10 A.M. She pressed the stop button and jumped out of bed.

"Coming, Dad! Be down in five!"

The nightmare had been *so* real! Sesame knew she was being silly, but she opened her special jewellery box, to check the charm bracelet was still inside.

168

It was. Eleven, glistening silver charms were fastened to the silver band, safe and sound. Happily she closed the lid and went to the window. It was a sunny Saturday morning and there wasn't a witch in the sky – just a fluffy white cloud, which Sesame thought looked like four-leafed clover. A lucky sign. And she would be riding her favourite pony, Silver, at Jodie Luck's stables in less than an hour.

"I can't wait to ride!" she told her teddy, Alfie.

Dashing to the bathroom to wash, Sesame told herself to stop thinking about Zorgan and his stories about the Silversmith. But ever since her last adventure in Karisma,✶ she couldn't help wondering if the Silversmith really *was* a wicked witch. No wonder I'm having weird dreams, she thought. She washed and brushed her teeth, then paused to look in the mirror.

✶ Do you remember what happened? You can follow Sesame's last adventure in Karisma in Book Eleven: *The Mirror of Deception*

"Nothing is going to stop me looking for the charms," she said. "I've only two more to find. Sesame Brown will track them down!"

A few minutes later, she was pulling on her jodhpurs, shirt and riding boots in record time. Then, remembering to put on her favourite necklace with a locket, she raced down to the kitchen.

✳ ✳ ✳

After breakfast, Nic drove Sesame to the stables. On the way they talked about the barbeque Nic had planned for that afternoon.

"I've texted Maddy, Gemma and Liz," said Sesame. "They can come."

"Great," said Nic. "I've invited some friends. They're looking forward to meeting Jodie. I can't believe we've been going out for nearly a year!"

"Brill," agreed Sesame. She was very fond of her riding teacher; for some time she'd been wondering

170

how she would feel if her dad and Jodie decided to marry. Sitting in the back of the car, Sesame started to daydream. Her mum, Poppy, had died when she was a baby, but she still felt loyal to her. It would feel strange to have a new mum around. Nevertheless, she found herself hoping Poppy wouldn't have minded about Jodie, because she *was* really nice . . .

Soon Nic turned off the busy road and drove down a rough track, flanked by neatly-fenced paddocks, to the stables. While he was parking the car, Sesame saw Olivia Pike – a girl she knew from school, who kept her own pony, Misty Morning, at Jodie's livery stables. Olivia was very snobbish and Sesame didn't like her at all. Her mother, Mrs Pike, was talking to Jodie and,

171

from the way she looked, Sesame could tell she wasn't happy about something. After a brief conversation Jodie hurried over to them, her soft blue eyes flashing with fury.

"Problems?" said Nic. He thought Jodie looked even more attractive when she was angry.

"Mrs Pike insists there's been a mix-up over Olivia's riding lesson," said Jodie. "She *says* she booked a lesson for ten o'clock. I checked. It was for eleven. But if I don't agree to change it, she's threatened to take Misty away and keep him at another stable—"

"The old witch," mumbled Sesame.

"Ses!" warned Nic. "Don't be rude."

"I've sorted it," said Jodie, "but I'm afraid you'll have to wait for your ride this morning, Sesame."

"That's okay," said Sesame. She was disappointed, but she knew it wasn't Jodie's fault. "I'll help around the stables while I'm waiting."

"Good," said Nic. "See you later. Don't be late for the barbeque. I'm cooking!"

Jodie gave him a quick kiss.

"I'll bring Sesame home," she said. "Don't worry. We'll be there in good time!"

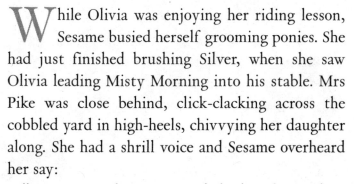

Two

While Olivia was enjoying her riding lesson, Sesame busied herself grooming ponies. She had just finished brushing Silver, when she saw Olivia leading Misty Morning into his stable. Mrs Pike was close behind, click-clacking across the cobbled yard in high-heels, chivvying her daughter along. She had a shrill voice and Sesame overheard her say:

"Hurry up, Olivia. I mustn't be late for my hair appointment. Raymondo is doing my highlights today."

"Yes, Mummy," said Olivia. "But I must give Misty some water—"

Mrs Pike looked at her watch.

"We haven't got time!" she said impatiently.

Sesame frowned.

"Mrs Pike is more concerned about her hair than caring for Misty!" she whispered to Silver, as she shut his stable door. It occurred to her that maybe Mrs Pike had wangled an earlier lesson for Olivia, so *she* could get to the hairdressers. A few minutes later, she watched them roar off in a four-by-four, leaving clouds of dust. Jodie came over to Sesame, sighing with relief.

"Now you can have your ride," she said. "Shall we tack Silver up?"

"Er . . . I should water Misty first," said Sesame.

"Why?" asked Jodie. "Surely Olivia saw to him before she left?"

Sesame hadn't *meant* to get Olivia into trouble. Reluctantly she told Jodie what had happened.

"You wait till I see Mrs—" Jodie began, and then stopped.

They heard a clatter of hooves on the cobbles and saw a pony bolting across the yard.

"It's Misty!" cried Sesame.

"He's making for the road!" shouted Jodie.

Sesame pelted after the runaway pony, taking a shortcut across a paddock. She reached the end of the drive in time to see Misty Morning disappearing behind a hedge near the road.

"Misty! Come back," she yelled.

Next instant, she heard the blare of a car horn, the squeal of tyres, someone shouting. Sesame skidded round a corner, her heart thudding. The traffic had come to a halt and, to her immense relief, she saw Olivia's pony standing by the hedge – his dappled-grey coat damp with sweat, eyes wide with fright.

Keep calm, Sesame told herself, as slowly she approached him. "It's okay, Misty," she said softly. "Stay. *Please* stay . . ." Suddenly Misty threw up his head and looked as if he was about to bolt again, when Sesame grabbed him by the mane. Which was when Jodie came running up with a halter.

"Well done, Ses!" she said, as they walked him back to the yard. "I couldn't have managed without you."

It took a while for them to settle the pony in his stable, so there wasn't time for Sesame to ride. Jodie promised to arrange another lesson very soon, then she rang Mrs Pike on her mobile.

"*So* sorry to interrupt your hair appointment," she said. "But there's something we should talk about . . . NOW!"

✳ ✳ ✳

They arrived at Sesame's house after everyone else, and found the garden full of people. Jodie caught sight of Nic squirting water on the barbeque flames. He waved to them through a haze of smoke and Jodie hurried off to help him.

Sesame spotted her friends by the apple tree, and raced across the lawn to greet them.

"Hi, Ses," cried Gemma.

"We thought you weren't coming," said Liz.

"We've been here *ages*," complained Maddy. "Only joking – *I'm* the one who's usually late!"

Sesame gave her best friend a hug.

"Sorry," she said. "Jodie and I had stuff to do at the stables."

Then she noticed her friends were wearing funky shorts, skirts and tops.

"I'll just change out of my riding gear," she said. "I won't be long—"

She was turning to go, when she was distracted by a prickling sensation at the nape of her neck. She held her locket and felt its familiar tingle, the way it did when something extraordinary was about to happen. Butterflies tickled her tummy. Goose pimples prickled her arms. Sesame saw pink, green and blue wisps of smoke, coiling and curling into a misty rainbow, swirling faster and faster, until her head was spinning and she felt her feet leave the ground. The others were caught up in it too and she heard their voices, floating to her from a distance:

"What's happening?"

"I'm flying!"

"I feel *weird*!"

The last thing she remembered was Maddy grabbing her hand, before they all floated up through the branches of the apple tree. Soon they were flying over the rooftops, whisked through the air on a magical rainbow, to the amazing world of Karisma.

Three

Zorgan had been in a foul temper ever since he'd failed to fool Sesame with his twisted stories about the Silversmith. She had stubbornly refused to believe him and secretly, he admitted to himself she had courage, but he had no intention of giving up.

"I'll find a way to break her will," he stormed over and over again. "Just wait till she returns!"

While the magician was waiting, he amused himself by inflicting spells on the innocent, unsuspecting people of Karisma: snowstorms on a summer's day, for example, and frightening nightmares.

It cheered him to see their discomfort. He was particularly pleased with a plague of mice he'd conjured, which had invaded the palace. Zorgan enjoyed observing them through his crystal ball;

the rodents were running amok in the royal household, causing no end of trouble. But the day before Sesame and her friends arrived in Karisma, he learned some disturbing news . . .

Queen Charm had called a Kluster,* to discuss the worsening state of affairs. Among her officials were the Chancellor, a stout man called Robustus, and Officer Dork; also there was Zorgan's old enemy, the Silversmith. Through the power of his magical sphere, Zorgan overheard every word . . .

"Zorgan is causing mayhem with his magic, Your Majesty. The palace is alive with mice! I found one in my soup today. Ugh!"

"Yes, the magician is making our lives a misery. I've been having terrible nightmares. Scary they were. It's time for action!"

"Sesame had a lucky escape last time she was here. I dread to think what Zorgan will try next. He's determined to get hold of the charms . . ."

* *

*Kluster – a meeting of important officials

"We shall do everything we can to protect your Seeker, Silversmith. My gatekeepers are on the look-out for Sesame and will help her in any way they can. In the meantime, the magician remains a threat. I had hoped we could resolve things peacefully. But enough is enough! Zorgan MUST be punished. Officer Dork, take him by force without delay!"

Zorgan couldn't believe his ears.

"Foolish queen!" he screamed at his crystal ball, as if Charm could hear him. "You dare to challenge ME? Dork doesn't stand a chance against my magical powers."

Nevertheless, Charm's words had given him cause for concern. Zorgan paced the floor of his Star Room, considering what to do.

"Forewarned is forearmed," he muttered. "I mustn't risk anything ruining my plans. When I have the fabulous bracelet, I'll empower it with Dark Magic. Morbrecia will become queen and wear it, but *I* shall control the charms and rule Karisma!"

182

He paused to look out of a window. Away in the distance was Heartmoor, where the Gorsemen lived, and it gave him an idea.

"I could make use of those prickly savages," he told Vanda, his pet bandrall.* "I'll send them after Officer Dork and his men. The soldiers will run for their lives when they see a hoard of Gorsemen charging at them! Come, Vanda, we're off to the moor. I shall go in disguise. From now on I can't be too careful. . ."

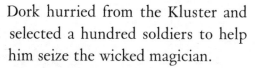

Dork hurried from the Kluster and selected a hundred soldiers to help him seize the wicked magician.

"We must be prepared for trouble," he told them. "You never know what to expect with Zorgan. We'll take the cannon. It hasn't been used for years, so it might be a bit rusty. Make sure it's in good working order and take plenty of mortar-melons."**

* Bandrall – rare flying mammal, native to Karisma
** Mortar-melons – ripe, round watermelons, traditional ammunition fired from Karisman cannon (mortar)

183

A soldier clicked his heels and saluted.

"Orders understood, sir!" he said.

For the next few hours, the palace was a scene of feverish activity, with everyone focused on the important task ahead. The soldiers cleaned the buttons on their uniforms and polished their boots till they could see their reflections in the toecaps. A gleaming cannon was mounted on a horse-drawn carriage, and several carts were loaded with melons.

By dawn the following day, the troops were assembled and ready to march.

Before they left, Queen Charm gave a rallying speech to speed them on their way:

"I have no doubt that dangers and difficulties lie ahead, but I am confident you'll succeed in your mission. Beware! The magician will be up to all kinds of tricks to avoid capture, but too much is at stake to allow Zorgan to remain free. The future happiness of Karisma rests with Sesame Brown and her quest to return my charm bracelet. Zorgan will do anything to get hold of it. Were that to happen, the consequences would be unthinkable! So, let no one stand in your way to bring the magician down. He must be caught at all costs! Setfair,* good soldiers. Have courage. May the luck of my charms, wherever they may be, go with you!"

* *
*Setfair – goodbye and good luck

185

Four

Sesame, Maddy, Gemma and Liz floated through the air, light as thistledown. For a while, they drifted over a bleak heart-shaped moor where nothing much grew except clumps of gorse; the bright, butter-yellow gorse flowers added colour to the landscape like splashes of paint on a picture.

Soon the girls were gently spiralling down to a rocky hill, where they landed near a cottage on the top. It seemed only seconds ago that they had been standing in Sesame's garden, and now they were worlds away in Karisma! The girls stood up and looked around.

Liz pushed her glasses firmly on her nose; everyone felt a little shaky. They appeared to be alone, apart from some speckled birds with long beaks and spiky crests near the cottage.

"I wonder where we are?" said Gemma.

"Heartmoor," said a voice right behind them.

The girls spun round, surprised to see a tiny, grey-haired woman who had appeared from nowhere. She had beady eyes, a beak-like nose and wore a ragged dress; perched on her head was a hat of feathers and over one arm she carried a basket. She shook Sesame warmly by the hand.

"Fairday,* Seeker Sesame," she said. "I'm Hesta the hermit, Gatekeeper Twelve. I've been expecting you."

How strange, thought Sesame. How did she know I was coming? I suppose anything's possible in Karisma! She greeted Hesta politely and introduced the others:

"These are my friends, Maddy Webb, Gemma Green and Liz Robinson."

"Hi," said Maddy.

* *
Fairday – a typical Karisman friendly greeting

"Great to be back," said Gemma. "It's ages since we were here together."*

"Yeah," said Liz. "We're all Charmseekers."

"*Four* Charmseekers," said Hesta, as if the number was significant. "A good sign. Sit down. I have much to tell you."

While the gatekeeper seated herself on a bench, the girls sat around on the grass, eager to hear what she had to say. It was the summer mede of Mima, and the afternoon sun felt warm on their backs.

* *
*✶ Do you remember when? You can follow the Charmseekers' exciting adventure in Book Eight: *Secret Treasure*

Hesta fed crumbs from her basket to the crested birds they'd seen earlier, then looked at Sesame with mock severity.

"Things have taken a turn for the worse, since your last visit," she began. "I'm afraid it's all your doing, Sesame Brown!"

"Oh!" cried Sesame. "What have I done?"

Hesta smiled.

"It's what you *haven't* done that matters," she said. "Zorgan is furious because you refused to bring him the charms. Brave girl! But he's taking it out on us. Him and his wretched spells!"

"What spells?" asked Maddy.

"Let me see," said Hesta. "A palace full of mice; a freak blizzard. Oh, and everyone's complaining about nightmares—"

"Ah," said Sesame, and she quickly told everyone about the one she'd had. "I guess Zorgan was responsible for that too."

"You *must* find the remaining charms," said Hesta. "The sooner Queen Charm has her bracelet back, the better. Only then will order be restored."

"We're looking for two more charms," said Sesame. "The cloverleaf and the key."

"I wonder which one we'll find first?" said Maddy.

Hesta had an inkling and replied in a riddle:

"Threes you'll see, the common kind;
The rarer fours are hard to find.
In flowery fields, 'tis my belief –
You'll spot the lucky . . .

". . . cloverleaf!" chorused the girls, jumping to their feet. She had given them a brilliant clue and they couldn't wait to start.

"Come on," said Sesame. "Let's go."

"Take care!" warned Hesta. "We are living in dangerous times. Her Majesty has ordered Officer Dork to capture Zorgan. The soldiers set out from the palace this morning. Zorgan will resist. He'll use curses, jinxes and all sorts to protect himself. It'll be quite a battle."

"Ooo!" said Maddy. "I hope we don't get zapped by a jinx."

Hesta rose to her feet and wished them well. She was halfway to her cottage, when Gemma remembered the gate and chased after her.

"What time do we have to be back?" she asked.

The gatekeeper pointed to the birds.

"Look for my friends," she said. "Return before you see twelve on my roof."

190

Five

Fearfully the Gorsemen watched the approach of an ominous dark cloud. They huddled in groups, each standing about four logs* high – about the height of a medium-sized troll; with their plump green bodies covered in prickles, they resembled a gathering of gooseberries.

* *

*Log — the length of a log is used as a measurement in Karisma – equal to about 50cms in our world

191

The cloud suddenly twisted itself into a tornado – a violent whirling monster, travelling towards them at alarming speed. The force of the wind nearly blew them off their feet. Two Gorsemen, in particular, were scowling at the sky – their names were Craggs and Spiker. As the tornado drew near, they saw a face emerge from the gloomy mass.

"It's Zorgan!" said Craggs.

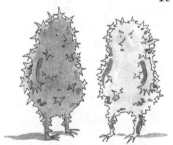

"What does *he* want?" growled Spiker. "Haven't seen the vermy* magician since he put a curse on us."

* * * * * * * * * * * * * * *
✷ **Vermy** – miserable worm

192

"Why *was* that exactly?" said Craggs. "It's so long ago, I've forgotten."

"Zorgan once pricked his finger on a gorse bush," said Spiker, keeping his voice low. "There happened to be some Gorsemen about, so he cursed us all with prickles. Horrible itchy things they are too!"

By now, Zorgan the tornado was hovering overhead, his voice thundered down to the Gorsemen below:

"There's work to do, my prickly friends! Do it well and you shall be rewarded."

"Hm! I wonder what sort of work *that* would be?" murmured Craggs.

"I think we're about to find out," said Spiker. "Here he comes."

Craggs and Spiker watched Zorgan spiral to the ground and shapeshift into himself.

"A slight misunderstanding with the queen," said Zorgan.

"Charm has ordered Officer Dork and his men to . . . apprehend me. A ridiculous plan! But I'm sure I can rely on you to see them off."

This met with a good deal of disgruntled murmuring among the Gorsemen, until Spiker ventured to say:

"You mentioned a *reward*—"

"Quite so," said Zorgan. "Defeat Charm's soldiers and I'll lift my curse. A bargain, you'll agree?"

The Gorsemen weren't happy with the idea, but the thought of being relieved from their irritable skin condition *was* tempting. And so the deal was struck.

"Good, good," said Zorgan. "Prepare for battle straightaway. Oh, just one more thing. Keep your eyes open for a girl. She's an Outworlder.* I'm offering a handsome reward to anyone who brings me Sesame Brown!"

The following day, as a stream of Gorsemen left Heartmoor, on their way to ambush Dork's troops, Sesame and her friends were setting out to charm seek.

* *
* Outworld — the name Karismans call our world

"Where shall we start?" said Maddy.

"Look for some flowery fields," said Sesame, remembering the gatekeeper's riddle. "In flowery fields, 'tis my belief—"

"You'll spot the lucky cloverleaf!" sang out Liz and Gemma.

As they walked along, Sesame told her friends what had happened the last time she was in Karisma. It was a good opportunity to catch up on Charmseeker news. When Sesame got to the part where she went to Zorgan's Tower and came face to face with the magician, they all gasped.

"Oh, Ses!" cried Maddy. "You were SO lucky to escape."

"I know," said Sesame. "I was scared. Morbrecia was there too. She was really nice to me, so I suspected something weird was going on. In a funny way I feel sorry for her. After all she *is* the eldest sister. She's mad because Charm is queen. And I'm still not sure about the Silversmith . . ."

"I remember, you had a nightmare about *her*," said Gemma.

"We know loads of stuff about the Silversmith making the charms," said Liz. "If only we could see her."

"That's the problem," said Sesame, "I think I *did*. She was the beautiful woman in my nightmare with long, silvery hair and sparkling eyes.

195

But when I gave her the charm bracelet, she turned into a horrid witch!"

They had reached the edge of the moor and stopped to look around. Drifting overhead were some puffy white clouds. Sesame told the others about the one she'd seen from her window that morning, shaped like a cloverleaf.

"I knew it was a lucky sign," she said. "I'm sure we'll find the charm soon."

There was a faint smell of coconut from the gorse flowers in the air and, not far off, they saw fields of purple clover.

"Flowery fields!" chorused everyone happily, jumping up and down with delight.

"Great," said Sesame. "I'll race you there!"

Meanwhile, a band of Gorsemen (which included Craggs and Spiker) had been trundling over the clover fields; some were pushing handcarts full of gorse balls,* while others were struggling with a strange-looking piece of equipment on wheels. It was a catapult, designed to hurl flaming gorse balls over a considerable distance; it looked like a giant wooden spoon attached to ropes and pulleys, and it was called 'The Fiery Flinger'.

* *
✱ **Gorse balls** – buds of the native Karisman gorse, which grow into large, spiky balls

However, the difficulty of manoeuvring the heavy contraption over ruts and hummocks, coupled with the itchiness of their skin, made the Gorsemen tired and crotchety, so they sat down to have a rest. Which is when they spotted four girls running their way . . .

"Vixee!" * exclaimed Spiker. "Outworlders!"

"Zorgan only mentioned one," said Craggs. "What was her name? Sumsunny Down . . ."

"Sesame Brown!" said Spiker. "But which one *is* Sesame? We don't know what she looks like."

"Ah," said Craggs. "I hadn't thought of that."

"Well, if we want to claim Zorgan's reward," said Spiker, "here's what we'll do . . ."

Clover grows tall as corn in Karisma, and soon the girls were waist-high in a sea of purple flowers.

"It'll take *ages* to find the charm in this lot," said Gemma, parting a way through the stems.

"I think someone's been here before us," said Maddy. "Look – wheel tracks."

* *

* **Vixee** – a gleeful, triumphant exclamation meaning 'great' or 'wicked'

The others saw where she was pointing.

"Some sort of cart by the looks of it," said Sesame, examining the freshly flattened plants.

"I wonder who— " began Liz and stopped.

They all heard a rustling noise, close by.

"Who's there?" they shouted.

There followed the sound of dry stalks snapping, and suddenly Sesame, Maddy, Gemma and Liz found themselves surrounded by Gorsemen. The bristly, green men looked most unfriendly, so the girls clung to each other for support.

"Which one of you is Sesame Brown?" Spiker demanded, his tone threatening.

Sesame was about to step forward, when Maddy held her back.

"I am!" declared Maddy boldly.

Immediately, Liz and Gemma cottoned on.

"No, I am," said Liz.

"It's me," said Gemma.

Sesame knew her friends were trying to help, but she couldn't let them take her place.

"*I'm* Sesame Brown!" she said firmly.

Spiker looked confused, until Craggs came up with a suggestion:

"I think it's the first one," he muttered.

"Right," whispered Spiker. "When I give the signal, grab her!"

While the Gorsemen were talking, the girls were plotting their next move.

"Let's make a run for it," said Sesame, keeping her voice low. "We'll split up to confuse them."

"Good idea," agreed Maddy.

"Okay," said Gemma and Liz.

"Ready," said Sesame.

"One, two, three . . . GO!"

At the very same moment, Spiker signalled to the waiting Gorsemen.

"After her!" he yelled.

And they tore after Maddy like a pack of hounds.

Hidden in the Clover

Can you find these nine words
hidden in the clover field?
Look for the words down, across,
diagonally and backwards.

SESAME

MADDY

GEMMA

LIZ

CLOVERLEAF

CHARM

SPIKER

CRAGGS

GORSEMEN

S	C	C	H	A	M	M	Y	P	E
E	L	S	G	G	A	R	C	M	I
M	O	A	A	C	D	D	A	Y	Z
A	V	M	L	C	H	S	O	V	M
S	E	I	I	Z	E	A	G	G	A
O	R	K	Z	S	M	K	R	Y	D
F	L	E	A	M	M	E	G	M	D
R	E	P	G	V	Z	I	R	A	Y
A	A	G	O	R	S	E	M	E	N
M	F	S	E	S	P	I	K	E	R

Six

In his Star Room, Zorgan peered through his powerful telescope, keeping a watchful eye on everything. He had witnessed the arrival of Sesame and the Charmseekers. He knew Craggs and Spiker would be tempted by a reward, and was sure it was only a matter of time before they delivered Sesame to his door.

In the meantime, he was pleased to see a large number of Gorsemen heading towards the tower, ready to defend him. Zorgan chuckled, thinking how easily he'd tricked them into believing he could lift the curse.

"The Prickly Curse is irreversible," he told his pixies, Nix and Dina, who were standing nearby. "By the time the Gorsemen learn the truth, it will be too late. If they cause trouble, I'll zap them with a spell. *Poof!* Bye bye, Gorsemen. Prickles and all!"

The pixies knew how ruthless the magician could be and stood there quaking in their shoes.

"You are very powerful, Master," said Nix.

"No one would dare challenge *you*," said Dina.

"Hm! Well, Queen Charm has done that very thing," said Zorgan. He swung the telescope in the direction of the palace. He could see a brigade of soldiers, their helmets glinting in the sunlight, marching his way. He was surprised at how many there were. A cruel smile curled his lips.

"Nix. Dina. Bring my spell books," he said. "Just Jinxes by Professor Brimstone and A Cauldron of Curses by Wizard Wanditch. Then let the fun begin!"

Shortly afterwards, there was a knock at the tower door. Zorgan opened a window and looked down to see Craggs and Spiker. They were standing by a handcart, looking very pleased with themselves.

"We've got Sesame Brown!" they shouted up to him.

"Spallah!" ✷ cried Zorgan. "I knew I could rely on you."

So he ran down one hundred and ninety-five twisty steps and opened the door . . .

Maddy had spent an extremely unpleasant and uncomfortable journey in the handcart. Gagged, bound and lying under a heap of gorse balls, she had been jabbed so many times she felt like a pincushion. Suddenly the cart upended and she was dumped like a sack of coal on the doorstep. Craggs and Spiker proudly presented her to Zorgan, but they were shocked by the magician's reaction. He looked furious.

"Magworts!" ✷✷ Zorgan fumed. "You've got the wrong one!"

✷ ✷

✷ Spallah – excellent! a triumphant expression

✷✷ Magwort – probably the worst name you could call anyone! General term for a fool

Maddy, now lying helpless on the ground, watched as sparks flew from Zorgan's wand; the jinxes singed the Gorsemens' prickles. Craggs and Spiker hopped around yelping.

"Ouch!"   "Stop it."

"Oooo!"   "That hurt!"

Then everything happened at once. Maddy suddenly found herself bundled into the tower, along with Craggs and Spiker. She was vaguely aware of Nix and Dina; Zorgan was shouting and the pixies were obeying orders. They freed her from the ropes, then locked her in a room with the Gorsemen. When they had gone, Maddy tore off her gag and confronted her prickly companions.

"This is all your fault!" she said crossly.

"But you *said* you were Sesame," complained Craggs.

"Yeah, how were we supposed to know you weren't?" said Spiker indignantly. He rubbed his head where Zorgan had scorched him with a jinx. "You shouldn't tell lies."

"And maybe you shouldn't go around kidnapping people!" said Maddy.

For the next few minutes they glared at each other in silence. Maddy was angry and scared too, but she wasn't going to show the Gorsemen how she felt. She wondered where Sesame, Gemma and Liz were now. Would she *ever* see them again!

Craggs interrupted her thoughts.

"Zorgan promised us a reward for Sesame," he said miserably.

"*And* to lift his curse if we defended him," added Spiker, and told Maddy how all Gorsemen had come to be cursed. She couldn't help feeling sorry for them.

"How can you trust Zorgan after what he's done?" she said. "I bet he won't keep his side of the bargain. He's just using you."

Craggs and Spiker nodded.

"You may be right," they agreed.

The three then looked around for a way of escape.

 They appeared to be in a dungeon, at the foot of the tower. Spiker tried the handle of the heavy wooden door, but it wouldn't budge. The walls were made of stone, but in one there was a crack; a shaft of sunlight streamed through from the outside, and that gave Maddy an idea. She fished in her pocket and produced a handkerchief with her initials embroidered in one corner.

"Pass me the rope," she said to Craggs. "I'll tie one end to my hanky. Push it through the crack. Someone may see it and rescue us." She hoped it would be Sesame.

For the time being, there was little more they could do, so they sat and talked. The Gorsemen were curious about Maddy and her friends – they'd never met any Outworlders before.

"Why did you come to Karisma?" asked Craggs.

"Tell us about Sesame Brown," said Spiker.

"Okay," said Maddy. "Oh, I'm Maddy by the way. There's Sesame, she's my best friend, and Gemma and Liz. We're in a secret club called the Charmseekers . . ."

Seven

Meanwhile, back in the clover field, Sesame, Gemma and Liz were becoming worried about Maddy. They'd eventually met up, having escaped capture by the prickly Gorsemen.

"You know Maddy, she's always late!" joked Gemma, trying to cheer everyone up.

"Maybe she's found the charm?" suggested Liz, not very convincingly.

Sesame tried to smile but, deep down, she knew something terrible had happened to her friend.

"I've seen loads of green men making for Zorgan's Tower," she said. "I have a nasty feeling the two we met have taken Maddy there."

"Oh, no," gasped Liz. "Poor Maddy!"

"Let's go after her," said Gemma.

"*I'm* going," said Sesame decisively. "They've taken Maddy hostage because they think she's me. If anyone's going to take risks, it had better be me."

"What shall *we* do?" said Liz, wiping clover pollen from her glasses.

"Look for the cloverleaf charm," said Sesame. "Please. You must find it."

"Cool," said Gemma. "We'll meet here later. Take care, Ses."

They gave each other their Charmseekers' hand sign for luck, then Sesame dashed away.

For a while, Sesame followed in the wake of the Gorsemen, keeping well out of sight. Soon she skirted the Dark Forest, which lay to her left then, spotting a clear line of cart tracks, she made straight for the tower.

It wasn't long before she caught up with the last of Queen Charm's soldiers, marching briskly along a road. Bringing up the rear was someone she recognised at once. It was Officer Dork.

"Oh, no," groaned Sesame. "Just my luck."

Her first instinct was to hide. Dork had accused her of stealing the charms several times before and had even attempted to arrest her once. She was relieved when he greeted her cheerfully.

"Fairday, Sesame Brown!" he said, slowing his pace, so she could march beside him.

"Hi," said Sesame.

In the distance they heard explosions and saw bursts of orange light streaking across the sky.

"The battle's begun," said Dork. "We were expecting trouble from the magician. But we shall bravely face whatever dangers lie ahead. No place for a girl like you, eh?"

Sesame rolled her eyes and ignored his last remark.

"I think my friend Maddy has been abducted and taken to Zorgan's Tower," she said. "I'm on my way to rescue her."

Dork looked horrified.

"Who'd do a thing like that?"

"Some prickly green men—" she began.

Dork stopped dead in his tracks.

"P-p-p-prickly green men," he said. "D-d-do you m-m-mean G-G-G-GORSEMEN?"

"I don't know," said Sesame. "Anyway, whoever they were they really wanted me. But Maddy said *she* was me so they took her away by mistake."

213

Dork looked confused, but he was under strict orders to protect Sesame.

"Allow me to escort you to the tower," he said, with a click of his heels. "Officer Dork at your service!"

While they marched along, Sesame told Dork about the Charmseekers.

"We've only two more charms to find," she said. "Then I can return Queen Charm's bracelet."

"Her Majesty is looking forward to meeting you," said Dork. "She is relying on you to save Karisma!"

"I can't wait to meet *her*," said Sesame happily. "I saw Queen Charm on Agapogo Day.* I was running away from her sister! She's after the charms too, you know."

"Ah, Princess Morbrecia!" said Dork with a faraway look in his eyes. He had always been in awe of the queen's rebellious sister, and just a little afraid. "I think Her Highness is under Zorgan's spell. The sooner we deal with HIM the better!"

✳ ✳ ✳

* *
* Agapogo Day — a holiday in honour of Agapogo, the dragon of the Silver Pool. Do you remember what happened? You can read Sesame's adventure in Book Three: *The Dragon's Revenge*

From her castle that same morning, Morbrecia saw the soldiers marching northwards to the tower. She was going there herself and had ordered her footmen to make ready her carriage.

Earlier, Morbrecia had received a strange message from her enchanted doll, Elmo. Zorgan had given Morbrecia the doll when she was six years old and ever since, Morbrecia had refused to part with her. Zorgan had often used the doll as a way to communicate with Morbrecia, but today was different. Today, it wasn't Zorgan's voice she heard, or Zorgan's words tumbling from Elmo's lips. The voice was high, chillingly cold and clear, and the words were unmistakably Elmo's own!

"Zorgan, this day, shall be no more,
So hasten to the wizard's door.
Fly to where the wizard dwells,
His crystal ball and books of spells
Are there and for the taking.
Soon you'll be magic making!"

Eight

The battle was raging. Sesame, who was still in the company of Dork, arrived to find the tower surrounded by Gorsemen. They were hurling flaming gorse balls at the advancing soldiers with The Fiery Flinger, and the air was thick with smoke and heat.

Despite the danger, Sesame couldn't help smiling to herself as she thought of her dad's barbeque, and suddenly home seemed very far away.

The soldiers retaliated with mortar-melons, which they fired from a cannon; the melons smashed against the tower on impact and showered the Gorsemen with slushy goo.

Zorgan, meanwhile, was in his Star Room blasting Dork's men with one well-aimed jinx after another. Sesame saw bursts of brilliant light flash from his wand and watched, horrified, as one jinx found its mark. A soldier bending down to load another mortar-melon was painfully zapped on his bottom.

"Yeeeeeowooooo!"

screeched the unfortunate man.

However, when some soldiers were brave enough to recklessly charge at a band of Gorsemen, Sesame saw her chance to get to the tower. She charged with them, ducking and diving to avoid a hail of stinging jinxes, until she reached the door.

That was when she caught sight of Maddy's handkerchief, fluttering from a crack in the wall.

Sesame knew it must belong to Maddy; her initials, MW, were embroidered in a corner.

Sesame's heart thumped as she crouched low, to peer through the crack. A giant mortar-melon splatted against the tower and drenched her with slush.

"Maddy!" she shouted, above the noise of the battlefield.

"Ses!" came Maddy's immediate reply. "I can't believe you're here!"

"I'll get you out," promised Sesame. "But I have to see Zorgan first."

"Oh, Ses," said Maddy. "*Please* be careful!"

Down in the dungeon, although she knew Sesame couldn't see her, Maddy made their secret hand-sign and wished her good luck.

Dork's men rammed the tower door and smashed it to the ground. They had been wrestling with some Gorsemen and their hands were full of prickles. Sesame dashed past them and through the doorway. She sprinted up the twisty stairs and halfway up, she met Nix and Dina flying down.

218

"My master wants to see you," said Nix.

"Come with us," said Dina.

"Out of my way," Sesame yelled, pushing them aside. "I don't need your help."

She tore to the top of the tower and stood for a moment, breathless outside the Star Room. Her legs felt like jelly and her tummy was churning like a blender. She was scared – more frightened than she had ever been in her life – but she knew she had to confront Zorgan. She fingered her locket, held it for a second or two and felt it warm and tingly to her touch. Inside were the pictures of her parents, and thinking of them gave her courage. Then she pushed open the door and went inside.

Zorgan had his back to her, firing powerful jinxes from the window at the soldiers below. He screamed with delight when he hit one. Sesame stood rooted to the spot at the sight that met her eyes.

The Star Room was a fascinating place, full of weird and wonderful things for making magic; spell books, potions, a clockwork universe, flickering candles, a crystal ball . . .

Zorgan suddenly wheeled round and saw her standing there. His black eyes glinted.

"At last," he said. "I knew you'd come looking for your friend. Such loyalty is admirable in one so young— "

"Release Maddy!" demanded Sesame. "It's me you want, not her."

"Quite so," said Zorgan, pausing to fire yet another jinx from the window. There was a jet of light, followed by a **Bang!** and the distant howl of someone in pain. "But first we must strike a bargain. You will be familiar with my terms. I see you are wearing your pretty locket. Good. The very thing."

Sesame shivered. The magician's tone was creepy – like hairy spiders crawling down her spine.

"I'll free your friend in return for your promise," said Zorgan. "Swear on your mother's name you will bring me the bracelet!"

"No way!" shouted Sesame, finding courage she didn't know she had.

Zorgan was furious, his patience with this stubborn girl expired. He aimed his wand at her and screamed:

"Promise or you'll be sorry"

"NO!" yelled Sesame. **"NEVER!"**

There was a blinding flash.
An ear-splitting

Crack!

"Ooooof!" went Sesame as the jinx hit her locket like a thunderbolt. The force of it threw her to the floor. She felt the floor shake, the tower tremble. And then she heard the terrible wail of Zorgan in agony.

"Aaaargh! No. NO! This cannot be happening. I must . . . have . . . the bracelet. A thousand curses on you, Sesame Brown! AAAARGH—"

Dazed, Sesame struggled to her feet. She heard a *hiss!* and thought it was a snake. Nervously she looked around on the floor, but there was nothing there.

Where Zorgan had been standing, a pall of black smoke now coiled slowly upwards and out through the window. Zorgan the magician was no more. Sesame stood there shaking. She blinked and blinked, unable to comprehend what had happened. What *had* happened? she wondered. She wasn't sure. All she knew was that Zorgan had gone and somehow she'd survived the powerful jinx. She couldn't believe her luck.

Sesame raced back down the spiral staircase, two at a time. At the bottom she found Nix and Dina, frozen like statues and staring out at her from unseeing, crystal eyes. The pixies, who'd been created by Zorgan, could not survive without their master. Their steely wings would fly no more. Phew! I'm glad they won't be bothering me again, thought Sesame, as she ran outside.

The roar of battle had been replaced by loud cheering from both sides. She was trying to make sense of it all, when Maddy ran up to her and flung her arms around her.

"Ses! You did it. You did it!" she cried.

"Did what?" said Sesame, hugging her friend and wondering how she'd escaped from the dungeon.

Then everyone was talking at once.

"Zorgan disappeared in a puff of smoke!"

"Look. My prickles have gone!"

"Hooray! So have mine."

There was much laughter and back-slapping among the soldiers and the Gorsemen. They had lost their prickles when the curse magically disappeared with Zorgan. No one noticed a carriage drawn up at the side of the tower, nor the woman in a hooded cloak slipping inside. No one that is, except a little bird, and she flew away to tell the Silversmith.

Nine

Meanwhile, far away in the clover field, Gemma and Liz had been searching for the cloverleaf charm. It was like looking for a needle in a haystack.

"I wonder if Sesame's found Maddy?" said Liz, peering under yet another clump of clover.

"If anyone can, Ses can," said Gemma "Sesame Brown will track her down."

She stopped for a moment to look at a cloud.

"You won't find the charm up there," said Liz.

"Look," said Gemma. "See what I see?"

Liz adjusted her glasses and stared at the cloud.

"Well, I suppose it looks a bit like—"

"A cloverleaf!" said Gemma. "Remember what Sesame said? She saw one like it this morning. It must be a clue."

"Wicked!" said Liz.

The two girls ran through the field of clover, until they were standing below the cloud.

"Start looking," said Gemma. "We haven't been here before."

It took about another twenty minutes of crawling around on their hands and knees, before Liz yelled: "Found it!"

The perfect little cloverleaf charm was caught up in a tangle of weeds, glistening in the sun. Carefully Liz reached in and picked it up.

"Wow," said Gemma. "It's lovely."

They stood, taking it in turns to hold the magical charm, admiring its delicate design.

"Ses will be pleased," said Liz, proud to have been the one to find it.

Just then they heard voices calling to them.

"Gemma! Liz! Where are you?"

"They're back!" chorused the girls, recognising Sesame and Maddy's voices.

Liz clutched the cloverleaf charm in her hand, then together they raced across the field to meet them. They were astonished at the sight that met their eyes. There were Sesame and Maddy, riding on a weird machine on wheels, surrounded by the green men, who had caused all the trouble in the first place – only now the men no longer had any prickles and they looked very friendly.

Sesame and Maddy jumped down and hugged their friends.

"We've got SO much to tell you," she said, her eyes shining.

"And we've got something to tell *you*," said Liz, opening her palm.

"Yesss!" cried Sesame punching the air. She held up the silver cloverleaf for Maddy to see.

Maddy beamed, then she caught sight of the gatekeeper's cottage, high on the hill.

"The birds! We must get back to the gate," she cried.

Spiker stepped forward.

"I've got an idea," he said.

Minutes later, the four girls were sitting on the The Fiery Flinger, waiting for take-off.

"Ready?" shouted Spiker.
They took a deep breath.
"Fire!" yelled Craggs.

"Weeeeeeeeeee!"

screamed the Charmseekers, all the way
back to the gate.

"Hurry!" cried Hesta. "The gate is
closing."

Sesame, Maddy, Gemma and
Liz tumbled from the sky into
a misty rainbow, then they
were floating down, down,
down – light as feathers –
fluttering through the
branches of the apple
tree on to the lawn
below.

Nic was by the barbeque, brandishing a sausage on the end of a long fork.

"Food's ready," he called out to the girls, as if they'd been chatting for ages. "You must be hungry after all that gossiping!"

✻ ✻ ✻

Later that evening, after everyone had gone home, Sesame got ready for bed. She sat for a while in her room, thinking about what had happened. It had been an extraordinary day; she'd woken from a frightening nightmare, then there was the drama at the stables and it had ended with an adventure in Karisma. Sesame wondered how much longer it would be before she could tell her father, her grandmother, and Jodie – everyone who meant so much to her – about her secret, magical world. One day soon she knew she'd *have* to tell them . . .

She felt in her pocket and fished out the precious cloverleaf charm. The beautiful four-leafed clover nestled in the palm of her hand, glistening with a silvery light of its own. She recalled the gatekeeper's words, when they'd first arrived: '*Four* Charmseekers' she had said, as if the number meant something special. It did. Four *was* a lucky number!

The four of them had helped each other; Maddy had tried to protect her; Gemma and Liz had found the charm and, although she didn't really understand how, *she* had defeated Zorgan and helped everyone! It seemed too good to be true. She glanced in her wardrobe mirror, half-expecting a terrifying vision of Zorgan to leap out at her, but there was nothing there except her own reflection.

Sesame opened her special jewellery box and took out the silver bracelet; then she fastened the cloverleaf charm securely to the band and held it up to the light.

"Twelve magical charms," she told her teddy, Alfie. "Only one more to find and my quest is over."

She had just closed the lid, when her mobile jingled. There was a message from a number she didn't recognise.

Sesame switched off her mobile. Yes, she thought. It's been an amazing day.

Ten

"Officer Dork has told me everything," said Charm. "I can't believe Zorgan has gone forever."

"Destroyed by his own jinx," said the Silversmith. She allowed herself a wry smile. "I felt the shock of it myself. The jinx rebounded off Sesame's locket, which made it exceptionally powerful. Not even Zorgan could survive it."

"Quisto!"* exclaimed Charm. "I'm so thankful Sesame escaped unharmed."

It was the day after the battle at Zorgan's Tower, and the two women were walking in the palace gardens. They had entered the  maze and were walking along the narrow, grassy paths that went round in circles, until at last they reached the smallest circle in the middle. At the centre stood a large stone pot, planted with bright red poppies.

* *
*Quisto — an exclamation of surprise

"This is where it all began," said the Silversmith
wistfully. "This is where Sesame found your
bracelet with the heart charm, remember?"

"Of course," said Charm. "It seems such a long
time ago. Do you think Sesame will return my
bracelet soon?"

"I believe so," said the Silversmith. "She has only
one more charm to find. The little silver key, but—"

"But what?" said Charm, detecting a hint of
caution in her tone.

"Sesame still has to *find* the key, Your Majesty,"
said the Silversmith. "And dangers still lie in her
path. A little bird told me that Morbrecia has taken
possession of Zorgan's most dangerous spell books!

She has his crystal ball too. Your sister has always had a fascination for Dark Magic. I fear she may become a powerful sorceress."

Charm was shocked. She couldn't begin to understand how the Silversmith had learned all this about her sister, but the thought of Morbrecia making magic and mayhem was alarming, to say the least.

"It all started when Zorgan gave her that wretched doll!" she said.

"Elmo?" said the Silversmith. "I remember you telling me about her. You thought she tried to kill you!"*

"Yes," said Charm. "And *you* thought Elmo possessed supernatural powers. She's been a bad influence on Morbrecia, ever since. It would explain why she stole my bracelet. Why she's tried to stop Sesame finding my charms."

"I think Zorgan is to blame, not Morbrecia," said the Silversmith gently. "I don't believe your sister is really wicked or means you harm. She fell under Zorgan's spell when she was very young—"

"Zorgan *again*," said Charm, exasperated. "Will I never hear the last of that balam** magician?"

* *
* Do you remember what happened? You can read Charm's story in Book Four: *A Tale of Two Sisters*
** Balam – cursed, an angry exclamation

Later, when the Silversmith returns to her workshop on Mount Fortuna, she looks at the thirteen magic candles. The candle that bears the name of the cloverleaf has flickered and died. Now only one solitary candle glows, burning brightly for its missing charm.

"Where is the key? The key!" she whispers to the candle. She presses her fingertips to her temples, closes her eyes and focuses her mystic energies on her Seeker, far beyond the boundaries of Karisma. "Sesame must return and find the thirteenth charm. Then all will be well."

A million thoughts flit through her head like fireflies, and she knows what she must do. Few possess, as she does, the magic power to 'transworld'; she has transported herself to the Outworld once before and, when the time is right, she will go there again . . .

But that's another story! It must be told another day.

235

*For Fiona Kennedy — my editorial guide and mentor
on the quest — with much love and appreciation. A.T.*

KARISMA

CAPE CAT

CLOVER FIELDS

HEARTMOOR

DOLPHIN BAY

The Silver Pool

KEY POINT

SWAMPS

JUNGLE

MERMAID ROCK

BUTTERFLY BAY

One

One Saturday evening, shortly before her birthday, Sesame was at home with her grandmother, Lossy, watching television. She was engrossed in a programme about rescuing orphan orangutans. She thought the babies looked adorable, playing with their carers in a reserve.

"I wish *I* could look after an orangutan," she said, and suddenly a vision of Fig popped into her head.

He was the tiny tunganora* she'd
rescued, when she'd gone to
Karisma for the first time.
Sesame had last seen Fig and
his mother, Hob, after the Feast
of the Stolen Goblet,** and she
wondered how they were.

Lossy glanced at her granddaughter sitting on the
sofa cuddling her cats, Chips and Pins. She knew
how much Sesame loved animals and the TV
programme had given Lossy an idea. I'll go online
when Sesame's gone to bed and find out more about
it, she thought. Then she quickly changed the
subject.

"I expect Nic and Jodie are having a lovely
evening," she remarked casually.

"Mm," said Sesame. She sounded
enthusiastic. "Dad says he's going
to ask Jodie to marry him tonight.
He's bought a ring. I saw it
yesterday. It's gorgeous!"

* *

* Tunganora – a small ape-like animal with long, pink
shaggy hair, which feeds on the blue-spotted leaves of
the tuntree
**The Feast of the Stolen Goblet – gribblers perform
this ceremony, in which a powerful potion of leaves is
sipped from a goblet, reputed to be stolen from Agapogo

Lossy smiled. Sesame's mother, Poppy, had died when she was a baby and during the past year, Lossy had noticed a growing bond between Sesame and her riding teacher, Jodie Luck. A while ago, when Nic had asked Sesame how she *might* feel about having Jodie as her stepmother, she'd replied without hesitation: "Wicked!"

✻ ✻ ✻

Next day, Sesame, Nic and Lossy were discussing ideas for Sesame's birthday party. It was just two weeks' away and this year it fell at half-term, on Friday the thirteenth.

"Could I have a disco with a real DJ?" Sesame asked.

"Sounds great," said Nic.

"What about the noise?" Lossy said. "We don't want to upset Mrs Adams next door."

"If we give her plenty of warning, I'm sure she'll understand," Nic said. "I know a super DJ called Spinner Shindigs and we can have a marquee in the garden."

"*Thanks* Dad," said Sesame, her eyes shining with delight. "I've got loads of friends I'd like to ask. It'll be the best party ever! Don't worry, Gran. I'll go and see Mrs Adams. She's good fun. I'll invite her too."

Chips and Pins caught Sesame's excited mood and chased each other round the furniture.

"Okay," she said. "I won't forget you!"

Sesame got busy straightaway. First she wrote a guest list (quite a long one), then she designed and printed party invitations on her computer.

Please come to my
Birthday Disco Party
At Home on Friday 13th
7pm until late.
RSVP Sesame Brown
email: seekerSes@zoom.com

So, early on Monday morning Sesame was in the playground handing out invitations. There was one each for her special friends – Maddy Webb (her *best* friend), Gemma Green and Liz Robinson – and Sesame had specially remembered to invite Hayley, a new girl in her class.

"Thank you," said Hayley, her sea-blue eyes sparkling. She wore her golden blonde hair swept back with a hairband, like Sesame. "I love disco dancing!"

Sesame and Maddy sat near Hayley in class and they'd liked her at once. One breaktime, while they were chatting, Hayley told them a little about herself; she had a brown-and-white puppy called Snoopy, played the flute and loved collecting jewellery. When they heard about the jewellery, Sesame and Maddy exchanged glances; if only Hayley knew *they* collected magical charms! Maybe one day, Sesame thought, I'll tell her about our Charmseekers club.

Before long, Sesame was surrounded by a gaggle of girls, all chattering about her party and what they were going to wear.

When Olivia Pike came along, Sesame surprised everyone by giving her an invitation too. The whole school knew Sesame and Olivia were not the best of friends! But that was before an incident at Jodie's stables, when Sesame caught Olivia's runaway pony. Ever since, the two girls had been on friendlier terms. Maddy stared at Sesame open-mouthed.

"Wha—" she began.

"It's okay," whispered Sesame. "I'll explain later."

Olivia looked really pleased to be invited.

"Thanks, Ses," she said. "A disco with a real DJ? Wow. It'll be SO cool!"

Two

One morning on Mount Fortuna, the Silversmith wakes early, sensing there is something special about today. She throws off the coverlet, wraps herself in a gossamer robe and crosses the room to her window.

It is dawn. The fiery sun is beginning to rise over Mount Fortuna and already she can hear birds singing. The Silversmith looks at her calendar and sees that it is the thirteenth day of the thirteenth mede✶ of Quorus.

* * * * * * * * * * *

✶ Mede – month

"Of course," she murmurs. "Midsummer's Day. The most magical day of the year!"

Her thoughts fly to her Seeker, and for a reason she cannot explain, the Silversmith is sure this day will be special for Sesame too. She brushes her long, silvery hair, dresses, then hurries downstairs to her workshop to look at the thirteen magical candles. One by one, twelve candles have flickered and gone out – each one bearing the name of a precious charm: the heart, horseshoe, shell, cat, butterfly, snowflake, lantern, coin, star, dolphin, moon and, most recently, the lucky four-leafed clover. These charms, she knows, are safe with her Seeker in the Outworld.* Only one candle remains burning – a glowing beacon for the lost silver key.

"Last but not least," she says. "Sesame must find the thirteenth charm to complete the magical bracelet. Only then will order be restored to Karisma. The time has come for her to return . . ."

* Outworld – the name Karismans call our world

250

The Silversmith lights fragrant tinder-sticks of mystica* that fill the room with a spicy-sweet aroma. Placing her fingertips to her temples, she breathes deeply, then focuses her thoughts on Sesame, her jewellery box and the charm bracelet. Soon she is in a trance, summoning her mystic powers to transport herself – far beyond the boundaries of Karisma – to the Outworld!

*Mystica – an aromatic plant, native to Karisma. The petals produce a sweet smell when burned

251

Three

Sesame's birthday, Friday the thirteenth, dawned bright and sunny.

"It's going to be a fab day!" she sang, dancing round her room with Alfie, her teddy, swinging him round and round. Racing downstairs in her pyjamas, she found her dad and Lossy having breakfast in the kitchen. The post had arrived and there was a pile of birthday cards waiting for her on the table.

"Happy birthday, Ses," said Nic, hugging her tight. Lossy gave her granddaughter a kiss. "Just think, you're a whole year older!" she said.

Sesame munched her muesli and opened her cards at the same time. There was one from her aunt in Scotland, enclosing some birthday money.

"Brill!" exclaimed Sesame. "I've been saving up for the new Crystal Chix album for ages. Now I've got enough money to buy it."

"Here's my present," said Lossy, handing her a large, flat package.

"Ooo," said Sesame, opening it with care. "I wonder what's inside?" She took out a glossy brochure, a photograph and a certificate.

"Wow!" gasped Sesame, her big brown eyes open wide with excitement. "I've adopted a baby orangutan called Kee-Kee. Look, Dad, here's his photo. He's gorgeous. Oh, Gran, *thank* you!"

"What a fantastic idea," said Nic.

"I thought you'd be pleased," said Lossy.

Orangutan Appeal

CERTIFICATE OF APPRECIATION

Kee-Kee has been adopted by
Sesame Brown
In recognition of your kind
support and sponsorship.

Signed
Director,
Orangutan Rehabilitation Centre

For the next few minutes, Sesame's head was buried in the brochure reading about Kee-Kee. He was being cared for in a rehabilitation centre, just like the one she'd seen on TV.

LUCKY KEE-KEE!

Kee-Kee arrived in our Rehabilitation Centre on Friday the thirteenth – a lucky day for the orphan orangutan. She was found by one of our rangers, hungry and searching for food. Kee-Kee's mother was killed by contractors, who had been clearing the rainforest for palm oil development. Kee-Kee is four years old with long red hair. She weighs fourteen kilos and is very affectionate, full of energy and loves climbing trees. One of her favourite pastimes is having a bath. She splashes around and loves being cuddled, while she's dried in a towel.

Kee-Kee will be looked after in our centre until she's ready to be released into the rainforest, where she will continue to be protected.

Nic glanced at his watch and gave Lossy a knowing smile.

"Er, Ses," he began. "I'm afraid *my* present was a bit awkward to wrap—"

Sesame rolled her eyes.

"Dad, I don't mind. What is it?"

"It's . . . I mean . . . he's waiting for you at Jodie's stables," said Nic.

It took a moment or two for Sesame to take in what her dad had just said. She hardly dared believe what she *thought* he was saying.

"D-a-d—?"

"Get dressed for riding," said Nic. "We don't want to keep *your* pony waiting!"

Sesame sat in the car in a daze, repeating over and over again in her head the words – *your* pony!

She was still wondering if it was just a dream as Nic parked the car at the stables. Jodie was waiting in the yard with Silver, tacked up and ready to ride, and fluttering from his bridle was a gold rosette:

Sesame
Happy
Birthday!
Love,
Dad xx

Sesame was so excited she wanted to cry and hug them all at the same time. She flung her arms around Silver's neck, then hugged Nic and Jodie together.

"Here," said Jodie, eventually disentangling herself to produce a neatly-wrapped parcel. "You'll need this. Happy Birthday, Ses!"

A few minutes later, Sesame was proudly wearing a smart new riding hat.

"Thank you, Jodie!" she said, and gave her a kiss.

For a while, Nic and Jodie watched Sesame riding confidently round the sand school; and when Nic took a photograph, Jodie remarked:

"Sesame and Silver. They're made for each other."

Nic turned to her. Jodie was wearing his engagement ring and the diamonds sparkled in the sunlight.

"So are we," he said happily. "Now, I must go. There's a lot to do to get ready for the party."

Jodie blew him a kiss.

"We'll be back soon to give a hand," she said.

* * *

Two hours later, Sesame and Jodie arrived to find a bright pink van parked outside the house. It had Spinner Shindigs' Mobile Disco painted on the side.

"Ooo!" squealed Sesame. She had caught sight of a good-looking young man in skinny jeans and dark glasses, carrying headphones, speakers and sound equipment down the garden path. "He must be Spinner Shindigs, the DJ."

"Right," said Jodie. "And there's your dad halfway up the apple tree!"

Nic and a friend were busy stringing lights in the branches. He waved to them and nearly lost his balance. Jodie shook her head and laughed.

"I'm going to help Lossy with the food," she told Sesame. "You go and change. I'll see you later."

"Okay," said Sesame. "I must look glam for my party!"

She raced upstairs to her room. The first thing she saw was a photograph, propped on her dressing table – the one Nic had taken earlier.

"Silver, my very own pony," she said, still hardly able to believe it. Lying next to the photo was a picture of Kee-Kee, her adopted orangutan. She was proud of her too. Quickly she put the photos down, then opened her wardrobe door.

"What *am* I going to wear?" she said.

Her bedroom floor was soon strewn with clothes, shoes and accessories – silky dresses, mini skirts, jeans, tee-shirts, sparkly tops and sequinned sandals, not to mention the entire contents of her make-up bag!

Glitter nail polish, lip gloss, body glow and dazzle dust – to name but a few – littered the carpet. Eventually she decided on her bright red top with a sparkly heart,* purple mini-shorts and shimmering tights. Then she sat on her bed and put on her favourite necklace – the locket with pictures of her parents inside.

Unexpectedly, a terrifying image of Zorgan the magician suddenly swam into her head; she vividly recalled what happened the last time she was in Karisma. Somehow (she didn't know exactly how) her locket had saved her from Zorgan's powerful jinx. The jinx had struck like a thunderbolt and knocked her to the floor. There had been a blinding *flash*. An ear-splitting CRACK! She guessed the jinx must have bounced off her locket and hit Zorgan, because the next thing she knew, he'd disappeared in a puff of smoke. She could still hear his wail ringing in her ears.

As Sesame held her locket now, she was aware of a tingling sensation in her fingers. It was a familiar feeling, and it nearly always meant something extraordinary was about to happen! Butterflies

* *

*Do you remember what happened when Sesame first saw it in **Tip Tops**? Read about her exciting adventure in Book One: *The Queen's Bracelet*

tickled her tummy and something compelled her to reach for her jewellery box. It contained the precious charm bracelet. She opened the lid, took out the bracelet and admired the twelve magical charms fastened to the silver band.

"Only one charm still missing," she said. "I must find the key!"

Outside, Spinner Shindigs was testing his speakers. Sesame heard rhythmic beats and recognised the unmistakable sound of the Crystal Chix. But then she heard another voice singing and was sure it wasn't the CD. The sweet sound echoed inside her head like a thousand tinkling bells.

"Sesame, come find the key,
Take my hand and fly with me!"

Sesame closed her eyes and shook her head. Was she hearing things? When she opened them again, she saw her room bathed in the soft, golden glow of candlelight and she was floating above her bed! Slowly she drifted up, up, up, still holding tight to the charm bracelet, until the ceiling melted away into a mist of tiny, twinkling stars . . .

261

As if in a dream, Sesame felt someone take her gently by the hand. Through a shimmering haze, she saw a young woman with long, silvery hair and thought the beautiful stranger looked familiar. Sesame struggled to remember where she might have seen her before.

"Who are you?" said Sesame.

But her words were lost and all she heard was a tinkling echo.

"... fly ... fly ... fly with me!"

* Four *

The dawn sky was a blaze of pink, blue and gold as Sesame and the Silversmith drifted on a sunbeam, towards Mount Fortuna. They landed, light as thistledown, outside the Silversmith's workshop.

"Come in," she invited Sesame, opening the door. "We have much to talk about."

Still shaken and bewildered, Sesame followed her inside. Everywhere she looked were curious ornaments, carvings and sculptures; there were star charts, moon charts and drawings of the magical charms; neatly arranged on a workbench was an assortment of tools and, over by the window, was a row of candles – but only one was burning.

"Please, tell me who you are," said Sesame.

"I'm the Silversmith," the young woman replied.

"Are you a . . . gatekeeper?" asked Sesame.

"In a way," said the Silversmith with a smile. "I'm the last portal. I had to bring you here to find the thirteenth charm."

"The key!" said Sesame. "Look, I have the bracelet with me."

Sesame opened her palm and the Silversmith gasped.

"Oh," she cried. "The precious charms! How wonderful to see them again. Do you know, I made the bracelet for Queen Charm here in this workshop. I can't wait to tell Her Majesty. She's been longing for its return, since the day it was stolen. Today is a holiday to celebrate Midsummer's Day. It would be perfect to return the bracelet to her on this special day. Charm is looking forward to meeting you."

"I'd love to meet *her*," said Sesame. "After I've found the key."

"We're depending on you," said the Silversmith. "Let me show you something."

264

Sesame followed her across the room to the window.

"These are *magic* candles," said the Silversmith, and she explained how they worked. Sesame noticed the one  remaining candle bore the name of the key.

"I'll find it," she promised. "Sesame Brown will track it down!"

The Silversmith gave her a look filled with warmth and affection. She had chosen well. Her Seeker would see her quest through to the end. "I see you're wearing your locket," she said.

"Yes," said Sesame. "It has pictures of my parents. I'll show you."

She opened the locket and the Silversmith bent to look at the tiny photographs of Nic and Poppy.

"No wonder it means so much to you," said the Silversmith gently. "I'm sorry Zorgan and his pixies gave you so much trouble."

"You know about—" began Sesame.

265

"I have . . . special powers," said the Silversmith. "I have been able to communicate with you through your locket. I knew the instant you were parted from it and I felt a terrible jolt when Zorgan's jinx struck it."

"What *did* happen?" asked Sesame, amazed the Silversmith knew so much about her.

"It rebounded," said the Silversmith simply. "You were very lucky to escape unharmed. Your locket saved you and destroyed the magician.* A jinx striking silver is exceptionally powerful, you see. When it bounced back and hit Zorgan, he didn't stand a chance. Karisma is well rid of that vermy** magician, and we have you to thank for our good fortune."

Just then they heard a strange noise outside the window. *Whoop-whoop-whoop!* Sesame knew she'd heard it before and when she looked, there were Hob and Fig!

"SESAME!" cried the tunganoras, jumping up and down with delight.

* *

* Do you remember what happened? You can read about Zorgan's dramatic end in Book Twelve: *Zorgan and the Gorsemen*

** Vermy — miserable worm

266

Sesame and the Silversmith ran outside to greet them. Hob was carrying a box, which Sesame recognised at once.

"My lunch box!" she exclaimed. "I left it in the jungle. How did you find it?"

"It's a long story," said Hob. "We were looking for food near Butterfly Bay—"

"—And we saw this great . . . BIG . . . enormous Plod-puss-opussy!" broke in Fig excitedly.

Hob, Sesame and the Silversmith laughed.

"I think you *may* have seen a Plodopus," *
said the Silversmith.

"Anyway," said Hob, "Fig came across your lunch box. It was very useful for carrying the goblet."

"Goblet?" queried the Silversmith.

"The one the gribblers stole from Agapogo," **
said Sesame, opening the lid. "I took it away from them and now Hob and Fig have brought it to you."

* *
* Plodopus – this plant-eating dinosaur is believed to be a close relative of Diplodocus, which lived in the Outworld millions of years ago
** Agapogo – a favourite name for dragons, which means 'to spit fire'

267

"How wonderful!" said the Silversmith, holding up the fine silver goblet. "We shall return it to Agapogo straightaway. The Silver Pool is not far from here."

Hob and Fig were tired; they had walked all the way from the jungle. Fig was sucking his paws and Sesame knew it was a sure sign he was hungry. Suddenly an image of her adopted orangutan, Kee-Kee, swam into her head. She felt responsible for the tunganoras; they had kept their promise to look after the goblet, now she must help them.

"Are there any tuntrees around here?" she asked the Silversmith. "Hob and Fig are hungry."

The tunganoras looked at the Silversmith hopefully with their wide, appealing eyes.

"I've got some in my garden," she said. "Come along. You have done well. You're welcome to stay as long as you like. You'll be safe and there's plenty of food!"

Five

It had been a while since anyone had seen a gribbler* in the Dark Forest. The vile, fat, foul-smelling gribblers – their bodies covered in blobby warts, their sharp teeth a disgusting shade of yellow – had been frightened off by the Tree Spirits, soon after the Feast of the Stolen Goblet.

Three gribblers, Varg, Gorz and Bod had squelched across a marshy area known as The Swamps and reached the coast. Very few trees grew here and the gribblers were miserable – that is to say they were more miserable than usual, because gribblers are usually bad-tempered. At dusk one evening, as the light was fading, the biggest gribbler, Varg, was in a particularly disagreeable mood.

* *
*Gribbler – extremely unpleasant goblin-like creature with yellow teeth and bad breath

"Can't shee a shoshege in thish light," he said, squinting his hooded eyes and spraying his companions with slime.

"Can't find anything to eat in this place," grumbled Gorz. "I'm so hungry I could eat worms!"

"I just did," said Bod, the youngest. "I can feel them wriggling in my tummy."

The three had just reached the end of a narrow strip of land called Key Point, which jutted out into the sea. If the gribblers had any sense (which they didn't) they might have caught some fish, but they were far too stupid to think of it. Instead, they continued to peer at the ground looking for morsels of food, until Bod saw something silvery, glinting in a pool of moonlight. He stopped to pick it up.

"Washat?" said Varg, snatching it from him.

"I found it," protested Bod. "It's mine!"

Varg cuffed him round the ear.

"It's only a key," said Gorz, squinting at it with his piggy eyes.

"Itch a *charm*, shtoopid," said Varg, dribbling goo from his fangs. "Morbreeesha told ush to look out for charms, didn't sheee? We mush take thish to the princhess!"

An idea slowly formed inside Gorz's head. He drew back his lizard lips, showing yellowing teeth, and grinned.

"Maybe she'll give us a reward," he said.

"Well, let's go," said Bod.

But the gribblers had wandered into the territory of the Urchins – five skinny boys with slime-green bodies and flat, webbed feet called Tyke, Gumba, Lumsy, Lug and Fiz. The urchins spent their time beachcombing and regarded anything left lying about (which they called left-behindings) as their property.

"What have you got there?" demanded the tallest urchin, Tyke, appearing out of nowhere. "Who are you anyway?"

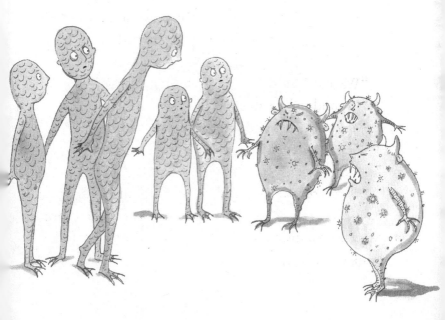

"None of your bishness," growled Varg, quickly hiding the key behind his back.

The urchins ducked to avoid the slime spray and held their noses too. The gribblers stank of rotting fish and the smell was unbearable.

"It is if you're stealing our left-behindings," said Gumba.

"Don't care if we are," said Varg.

"What are we waiting for?" asked Gorz.

"RUN!" cried Bod.

So the gribblers ran (hoping they were going in the direction of Morbrecia's castle) and the urchins chased them across The Swamps.

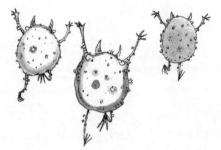

Six

Morbrecia's castle was crammed with books. After Zorgan's defeat, she had lost no time in raiding the magician's magnificent library. Morbrecia had loaded her carriage with spell books, then her servants had spent days putting them on bookshelves; and when those were full, they'd piled them on the floor. The princess couldn't wait to start making magic!

Most of Zorgan's books were for experienced magicians. Morbrecia was a beginner so, not surprisingly, she had a few unfortunate mishaps. Making potions, for example, is a bit like cooking. You follow a recipe, or the dish may be ruined. It takes time to become a good cook and it's the same with sorcery. If you make a mistake with magic, the results are disastrous.

The first leather-bound volume Morbrecia opened was A Pot Full of Potions. She'd selected a potion and, in her hurry, hadn't bothered to weigh the ingredients. A pinch of this, a handful of that – before long, Morbrecia had mixed a disgusting green and slimy brew. Alarmingly, the pongy potion refilled the cauldron, no matter how much she tried to empty it.

"Quick!" she yelled to her servants. "Fetch buckets, saucepans, bottles, jam-jars — *anything* to hold this horrid stuff."

By the time the magic had worn off, she had enough potion to fill a lake!

Now Morbrecia had also acquired Zorgan's crystal ball. Early on Midsummer's Day, as she was peering into the magical sphere she saw the Silversmith with Sesame, arriving on Mount Fortuna.

"Spallah!"* exclaimed Morbrecia. "Sesame is back and she's brought the bracelet!"

As usual, Morbrecia's doll, Elmo, was sitting nearby. Elmo possessed supernatural powers and now words tumbled from her mouth:

"Twelve charms she has, so you must scheme
To lure her here, then wait unseen.
A scary spider you shall be
Let's set a trap for Sesame!"

"What a good idea!" said Morbrecia, who needed no further encouragement. The thought of turning herself into a spider again was thrilling. It was how it had all started — Morbrecia the spider, stealing the charm bracelet from her sister. "I have the spell books.

* *
*Spallah — excellent! A triumphant expression

275

I have the know-how. Only this time I'll be stealing the bracelet from Sesame. The chance to snatch the bracelet is too good to miss! And then there's only the thirteenth charm to find . . ."

Wafting through an open window, Morbrecia caught a whiff of rotting fish. She looked out to see three gribblers, Varg, Gorz and Bod, scuttling across the bridge to her castle. Every now and then a skreel* leapt from the lake to snap at their heels.

"What do you want?" yelled Morbrecia, holding a hanky over her nose.

"We've got shumshing for you Morbreeesha," said Varg, holding up the tiny silver key. The charm shimmered with a light of its own in the morning sun.

"Vixee!"** cried Morbrecia, punching the air. "Come in."

She couldn't believe her luck. On the very day Sesame had arrived with the bracelet, the gribblers had brought her the last lost charm. She held the key, turning it this way and that, admiring its filigree design.

* *
* Skreel – small flesh-eating fish
** Vixee – a gleeful, triumphant exclamation meaning 'great' or 'wicked'

"Soon *I* shall be queen!" cried Morbrecia to her servants. They were exhausted from filling every available bucket and bottle with smelly potion, and had stopped to have a rest.

The gribblers sniffed the air with their warty noses.

"Lovely pong," said Gorz.

"Mmm!" said Bod. "Something smells delicious."

"What ish it?" asked Varg.

"Um, it's a potion—" began Morbrecia, an idea suddenly whizzing into her head.

"POSHUN!" said Varg, showering everyone with spit. "What short of poshun?"

"Oh," said Morbrecia, thinking quickly. "It makes you strong. Clever. And it helps you see in the dark!"

The gribblers dribbled with eager anticipation.

Morbrecia tried to hide a smile.

"As a reward for bringing me the charm," she told them, "please take the LOT!"

Seven

Meanwhile, Sesame and the Silversmith had left the tunganoras feasting on leaves in the Silversmith's garden. They were on their way to the Silver Pool to return the goblet to Agapogo. As they walked up the mountain, Sesame found herself chatting easily to her companion.

"I remember the legend of the pool,"* she said.

* *
* Do you remember the intriguing legend? You can read about it in Book Two: *The Silver Pool*

278

"The gatekeeper, Stanza, told us the story but that was ages ago when I was here with Maddy. She's my best friend, by the way. We felt SO sorry for the dragon. Poor thing! Imagine drowning in a pool of silver . . ."

The Silversmith smiled. Sesame was just as she'd imagined – friendly, caring, inquisitive and fun.

"I *think* you found the horseshoe charm that day?" she said.

"Yes!" said Sesame, and suddenly the perfect little horseshoe reminded her of Silver, far away; and then she thought of her dad, Jodie, her grandmother – everyone she loved – preparing for her birthday party at home.

For a split second she was torn between her determination to finish her quest and her longing to be there. She said quietly, almost to herself: "It's my birthday today."

"Ah," said the Silversmith. "I *knew* today was special for you too. Happy Birthday, Sesame!"

When they reached the pool, Sesame looked over the edge. Below them swirled a whirlpool of shimmering silver.

"Oh!" she gasped. "It's amazing."

"I made the magical charms from this pool," said the Silversmith. "It refills itself, no matter how much is used. It's a precious resource, so I try to use it wisely."

Sesame nodded, trying to take it all in. She thought the Silversmith must be very skilful. Fingering the charm bracelet in her pocket, she felt the charms warm and tingly to her touch. Is it, Sesame wondered, because they're close to the Silversmith, the one who made them? There were so many questions she wanted to ask, but now wasn't the time. The Silversmith was preparing to summon the dragon spirit!

Feeling scared, not knowing what to expect, Sesame clutched the goblet so tightly, her knuckles turned white. Fascinated, she watched the Silversmith close her eyes and sway, putting herself into a trance and softly chanting . . .

"Apost, Snargal, Incendus, Agapogo!"

Without warning, a terrifying wind got up and the force of it nearly knocked the two of them off their feet. Sesame braced herself against the blast. When she dared to look, she let out a startled cry.

280

The ghostly vision of Agapogo rose from the pool, her massive wings spread like sails, silvery scales glinting in the morning light.

"Don't be afraid," the Silversmith assured Sesame. "Agapogo will not harm you." She spoke in hushed tones and addressed the phantom respectfully:

"I bring good news," she said. "This is Sesame Brown. She is returning your stolen property."

Sesame gulped and took a step forward. The dragon spirit looked awesome! But she took a deep breath and held out the shining silver goblet.

"I th-th-think this b-b-belongs to you," she said. "I t-t-took it from the gribblers—"

Agapogo's hollow eyes lit up like hot coals at the sight of her long lost goblet. She snorted filling the air with scalding steam.

"Throw the goblet to her," said the Silversmith.

So Sesame tossed the goblet and Agapogo caught it in a claw; then the dragon spoke, her voice warm and gentle as a summer breeze:

"Good Silversmith and Sesame,
Kindred spirits in you, I see.
The thirteenth charm this day you'll find,
To evermore the bracelet bind.
A bond forever, as yours shall be –
Good Silversmith and Sesame!"

She sank into the silvery whirlpool, leaving a trace of bubbles on the surface. For a moment, Sesame and the Silversmith stood speechless, their feelings of happiness mixed with sadness. The dragon's words had given them hope for the future and Sesame was *sure* she would find the last charm – although she had no idea where to start looking . . .

The reflection of a doll suddenly appeared in one silvery bubble, which caught her eye. The Silversmith saw it too, and a shiver of fear ran down her spine.

"Quisto!"⋆ she exclaimed. "It's Elmo!"

Eight

"Who's Elmo?" asked Sesame. She guessed this was a clue from Agapogo, but what did it mean?

"The doll belongs to Morbrecia," said the Silversmith, and quickly told Sesame all she knew.

"A *magic* doll!" said Sesame, gazing at Elmo in wonder. "Perhaps Elmo knows where the key is. I must go to Morbrecia's castle and find out!"

"It's dangerous," warned the Silversmith. "Morbrecia has taken possession of Zorgan's most powerful spell books. Goodness knows what mischief she's up to! Wait. I'll go with you."

Sesame hesitated. She didn't know why, but suddenly she felt wary of the Silversmith.

"Er, thanks," she said. "But I have to do this on my own. I'm a Charmseeker, remember!"

"I understand," said the Silversmith gently. "But give the charm bracelet to me.

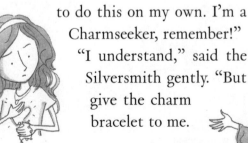

284

It would be dreadful if Morbrecia got hold of it. I'll meet you later at the palace."

The Silversmith's words struck Sesame like a bolt of lightning. *Give the charm bracelet to me.* She'd heard them before – in a NIGHTMARE! In it, Sesame had trusted a beautiful stranger, who'd looked just like the Silversmith. When she gave *her* the precious bracelet, she'd turned into a wicked witch!

Sesame didn't wait a second longer. Without a word, she ran from the Silver Pool and down the mountainside, faster than she'd ever run before.

The Silversmith sighed as she watched Sesame go. There was evil in the air, she could smell it!

Sesame didn't stop running until she'd reached the edge of the Dark Forest. She'd spotted Morbrecia's castle not far away; it loomed eerily out of the early morning mist, from an island in the middle of a lake. Sesame remembered the lake only too well — she and Maddy had once escaped the gribblers by racing across it on giant moon-lilies, dodging the deadly skreels!

She was about to set off again, when she heard the faintest flutter of wings behind her. Thinking it might be Zorgan's pixies, Nix and Dina, out to make trouble for her, Sesame spun round to confront them. However she was relieved to find herself face to face with a fairy, wearing a gown spun from fine cobweb. It was Quilla.

"Fairday,* Seeker," said Quilla, smiling sweetly.

Sesame thought she recognised the fairy and tried to remember where they'd met. Quilla knew what she was thinking.

"The market at Lantern Hill,"** she said. "You stopped to help me."

* *
* Fairday – a typical Karisman friendly greeting
** Lantern Hill – Do you remember what happened? You can read about it in Book Three: *The Dragon's Revenge*

286

"Quilla!" said Sesame, remembering. "A horrid troll set off a firecracker and you dropped a tray of potions. You gave me a pot of Vanishing Cream."

"Yes," said Quilla. "It helped you escape from Morbrecia."

They looked across to Morbrecia's castle.

"I'm on my way to see her now," said Sesame. "She may know something about the key charm. I must find it."

Quilla gave Sesame a knowing smile.

"Morbrecia is much misunderstood," she said. "Listen. I'll tell you a story, before you go.

"When Morbrecia was a child,
Zorgan's magic made her wild.
He took the princess for a fool –
Tricked her with his plans to rule.
So she, a spider, crept unseen
And stole the bracelet from the queen.
The plan went wrong. The charms were lost!
Now all Karisma bears the cost.
Go, Seeker, and you shall see,
Where the princess keeps the key!"

Before Sesame could thank her, Quilla disappeared. The fairy had simply vanished.

Nine

Midsummer's Day was a holiday in Karisma, as the Silversmith had told Sesame, and each year Queen Charm gave a Garden Party to celebrate. Invitations had been sent to all the guests, including the queen's twelve Gatekeepers. They had permission to leave their posts on this special occasion. Karismans travelled from far and wide to attend the party, and Charm welcomed this opportunity to get to know her subjects better.

The royal gardeners had been busy for weeks – planting flowerbeds, sweeping paths and clipping the huge topiary hedge. There were thirteen topiaries,

each one representing a charm on the queen's bracelet.

One gardener had even remembered to place a fresh pot of poppies in the middle of the maze. By Midsummer's Day, the gardens were looking their very best.

However, on the morning of the party, when the Silversmith arrived at the palace, she was far too anxious to notice the gardens. After Sesame's hasty departure from the Silver Pool, she had hurried to seek Charm's advice.

"I fear Sesame may be in great danger, Your Majesty," she said, wringing her hands. "She has your bracelet—"

"Oh!" cried Charm. She was thrilled to hear about her bracelet, but much more concerned for Sesame. "Where is she? What's happening?"

After the Silversmith told her everything, Charm took charge of the situation.

"Sesame must be protected from Morbrecia," she said. "My sister will do anything to get hold of my bracelet! And if she *does* know where the key is . . ." Charm twisted a strand of fair hair round her finger, contemplating the terrible consequences of Morbrecia in possession of the magical bracelet and *all* its charms.

"I'll send Dork to her castle at once!"

"I will go with him," said the Silversmith.

Party Time!

The twelve gatekeepers have been
invited to Queen Charm's garden party.
Can you send the right invitation
to each gatekeeper?

Etok, Cape Cat
Ramora, Star Island
Troll, The Dark Forest
Hesta, Heartmoor
Feenix, Lantern Hill
Quinch, Shell Beach
Pogg, Butterfly Bay
Stanza, River Two Moons
Ice Maiden, The Ice Country
Bogal, The Swamps
Selena, Mermaid Rock
Pogo, A Cave near The Coins

Solution: 1 Troll; 2 Stanza; 3 Feenix; 4 Etok;
5 Pogg; 6 Bogal; 7 Ice Maiden; 8 Pogo; 9 Ramora;
10 Selena; 11 Quinch; 12 Hesta

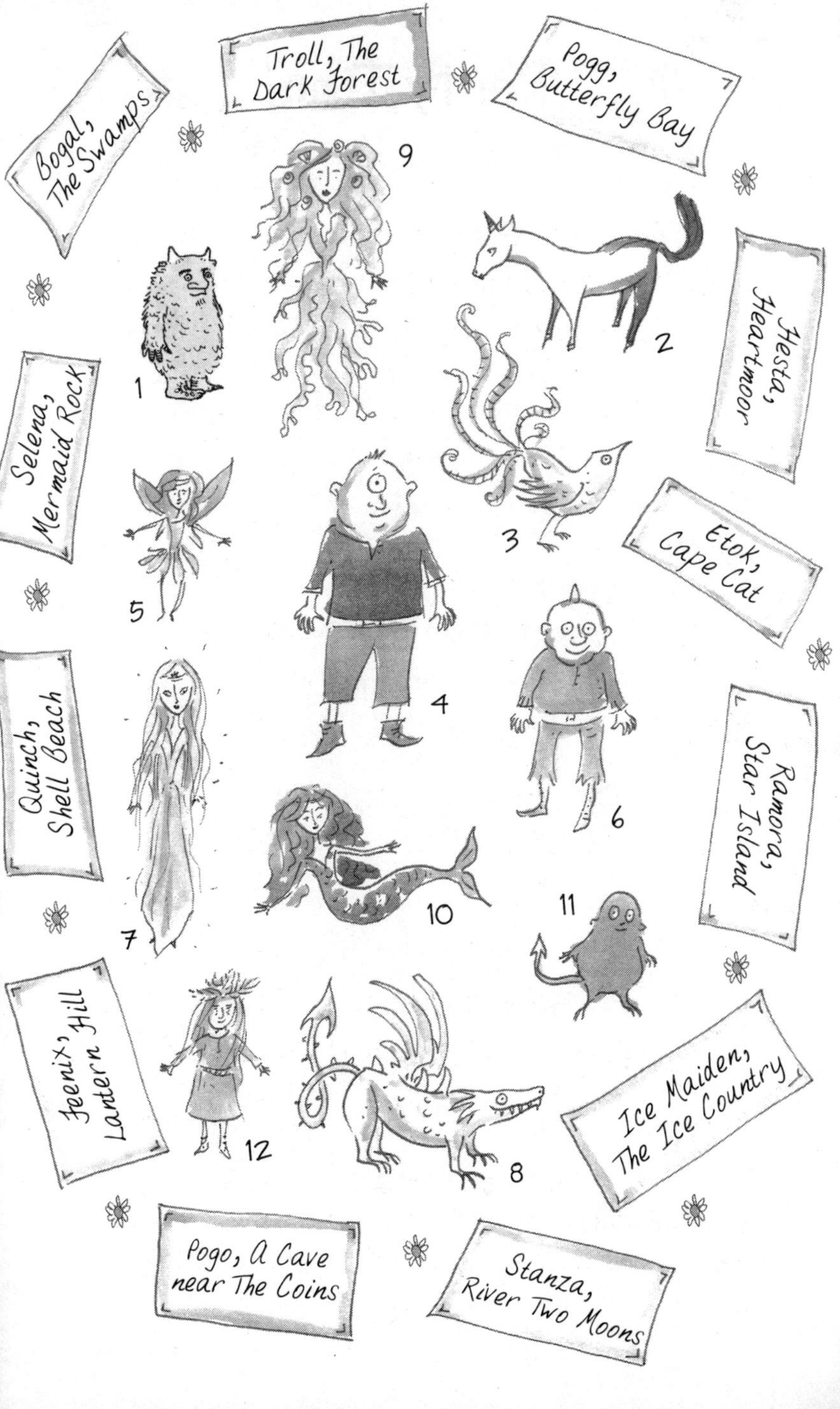
Bogal,
The Swamps
Troll, The
Dark Forest
Pogg,
Butterfly Bay
9
Hesta,
Heartmoor
2
1
Selena,
Mermaid Rock
3
Etok,
Cape Cat
5
4
6
Quinch,
Shell Beach
Ramora,
Star Island
10
11
7
Feenix,
Lantern Hill
Ice Maiden,
The Ice Country
12
8
Pogo, A Cave
near The Coins
Stanza,
River Two Moons

Sesame ran across the bridge to the castle. Every now and then she caught a whiff of rotting fish and looked nervously around for the gribblers, but there wasn't a sign of them anywhere. Sesame guessed they *had* been there but had gone, leaving their awful stench behind.

The castle door was wide open, so she stepped inside. What she saw next took her by surprise. In the great flag-stoned hall of the castle servants, coachmen and footmen stood around like statues – frozen as if they'd been playing some weird game of 'move and you're out'. Sesame went up to a guard and stood right in front of him.

"Hi!" she said, waving at him. "Anyone there?"

But there was no reply. The guard stared back, unblinking, as if she wasn't there. Spooky, thought Sesame, and her stomach turned several somersaults – backwards *and* forwards.

She felt alone and very afraid, and wished more than anything that Maddy was with her. And she regretted running away from the Silversmith. The Silversmith was being so *nice* to me, she thought miserably. I don't know what came over me. She must think I'm horrid and—

A sudden tingling at the nape of her neck jolted Sesame from her daydreaming. She felt her locket. It was unusually warm and the charm bracelet was vibrating — as if the two pieces of jewellery were uniting in their efforts to comfort her.

"Right," said Sesame, pulling herself together. "You're here to look for the key, so hurry up and get on with it. Sesame Brown will track it down!"

She strode across the hall to the foot of a narrow, twisty staircase to the tower and called out:

"Morbrecia! Are you there? It's me, Sesame. I'm coming up."

Her voice echoed round the castle walls. If Morbrecia was there, she wasn't answering. Sesame stepped on the first stair. It creaked. Step by step she went up, one floor after another, higher and higher, until she could go no further. There was one room in the attic and the door was ajar . . .

Sesame went in. The room was small and had a low-beamed ceiling tucked under the eaves; through a window she could see the lake sparkling far below. Everywhere she looked there were spell books, and potions fizzing in jars. A crystal ball was on a stand, and sitting in a rocking chair was Elmo. There was no sign of Morbrecia.

A scuttling sound overhead made Sesame look up at a thick wooden beam. At one end hung a huge cobweb; at the other, sat a spider – watching her every move. Sesame froze and words from Quilla's story flew into her head: *So she, a spider, crept unseen, and stole the bracelet from the queen . . .*

"Give me the bracelet," said Morbrecia the spider, "or I'll turn you into a fly. And you know what will happen then."

Sesame was terrified. But she wasn't going to give in so easily.

"No," she shouted, backing away. "Never!"

Morbrecia waved a spidery leg at Elmo.

"Now," she ordered. "Sesame, the fly. Ha, ha!"

The doll opened her mouth to cast a spell . . . and there, glistening on her tongue, lay the key!

Sesame gasped and lunged at Elmo shaking her, until the key fell from her lips. Then she flung her from the window. Sesame looked down at the lake and heard a dreadful *SMACK!* as Elmo hit the water. Almost immediately, the lake was alive with skreels, their razor-toothed jaws snapping at the doll. The flesh-eating fish worked themselves into a feeding frenzy, and for several minutes the water frothed and foamed.

Then all was still and quiet, as if nothing had ever happened.

Petrified, Sesame turned to look for the spider, but she wasn't there. Instead, standing in the room was Morbrecia – smiling and holding the key. Morbrecia felt as if she'd woken after a strange dream, although she couldn't remember much about it.

"Here," said Morbrecia the princess. "This belongs on Charm's bracelet!"

Ten

"Sesame!" came a shout from the stairs. It was followed by the sound of running feet and shortly afterwards, Officer Dork came into the room, puffing and panting.

"Are you all right, Sesame Brown?" asked Dork. "Princess Morbrecia, I'm arresting you for—"

Sesame stood protectively between Dork and Morbrecia, and behind Dork, she saw the Silversmith.

"It's okay," she said quietly. "Morbrecia and I are friends."

"Wha—?" began Dork.

The Silversmith gave a sigh of relief, happy to find her Seeker safe and Morbrecia back to her normal self. She had seen Elmo fall from the tower and with her, the last evil influence over Morbrecia. The princess was free at last.

"I understand," she said simply.

"I don't," said Dork, baffled. "Girls, eh!"

"I'll tell you later," whispered the Silversmith.

Sesame looked at the Silversmith, seeing now only her true nature. She would never doubt this kind and gentle person again. There was no need to explain; the Silversmith's smiling eyes told Sesame she knew exactly what she was thinking.

Feeling she could burst with happiness, Sesame quickly blinked away tears and fished in her pocket for the charm bracelet. Morbrecia, Dork and the Silversmith gathered round, as she fastened the beautiful filigree key to the silver band. For the first time since Zorgan cast the charms away on that fateful day, so many medes ago, all thirteen magical charms were together again!

"Three cheers for the charms!"

"Spallah!"

"Vixee!"

"Party time, I think," said the Silversmith. "Queen Charm is longing to meet you, Sesame. And she'll be over the two moons to have her bracelet back!"

"I can't wait to meet her," said Sesame.

"And I'm longing to see my sister again," said Princess Morbrecia. "I've missed her."

Morbrecia aimed a swift kick at Curses Ancient and Modern, which happened to be lying at her feet. "I won't be needing these spell books any more!"

A sudden breeze got up and ruffled the pages of the leather-bound tome. Then an odd thing happened; letters and words floated off the pages and out of the window like a swarm of flies. It was the same with all the other books from Zorgan's library. Chants, spells, jinxes and curses jumbled together and disappeared into thin air.

Meanwhile, down in the great hall, there came the sound of cheers and a great commotion. Morbrecia's servants had suddenly woken from a sleeping curse and were hurrying about their duties.

"Er, we should be getting back to the palace," said Dork. "Her Majesty's guests are arriving for the Garden Party."

"Yes," said the Silversmith. "Time to be off."

"We can all fit in my carriage," said Morbrecia.

But as they turned to go, Sesame caught sight of the crystal ball; she'd never used one and thought it might be fun. Morbrecia guessed what she was thinking.

"Have a go!" she said.

"Who do you wish to see?" asked the Silversmith, although she already knew the answer.

"My friends!" said Sesame excitedly. "They're coming to *my* party today. I wish they could be here to see the bracelet. They helped find the charms too. We're all Charmseekers!"

"I'll see what I can do . . ." said the Silversmith mysteriously.

Eleven

While guests were arriving at the palace for the queen's Garden Party, far away in the Outworld, Sesame's guests were arriving for her disco.

Maddy, Gemma and Liz arrived together early, and had thoughtfully collected Hayley on the way. The four girls squeezed into Mrs Webb's car, then chattered non-stop to Sesame's house about their sparkly outfits, bags, shoes and hair clips.

"Phew!" sighed Maddy's mother, when she dropped them off. "You'd all win gold medals for chatting in the Olympics! Have fun."

Jodie greeted them at the door. She'd been

helping Lossy with party food and had floury hands.

"Go on up to Sesame's room," she said. "She's been getting ready for *ages*. Tell her to hurry up."

They found the room in a mess, with Sesame's clothes all over the floor. Maddy was quick to spot the open jewellery box by her bed. She looked inside and gasped. The charm bracelet had gone – and so, it seemed, had Sesame.

"Ses!" she called out anxiously, looking around.

"What's the matter?" asked Hayley, who knew nothing about the bracelet, the Charmseekers or Karisma.

"Er, nothing," mumbled Maddy, not wanting to alarm their new friend.

"She's probably gone to the loo," said Liz.

"She'll be back in a minute," said Gemma.

But as the four girls sat on Sesame's bed to wait, the strangest things started to happen. First, the room filled with a golden glow, as if lit by magical

candlelight. Next, the girls felt light-headed and, before they knew what was happening, they found themselves floating above the bed and drifting up to the ceiling.

"Whoooooooah!" cried Hayley. "I'm flying."

"Me too," said Maddy, taking her hand. "Hold tight, Hayley. I've a weird feeling we're off to Karisma!"

Officer Dork escorted Princess Morbrecia and Sesame to the Garden Party in Morbrecia's carriage. The Silversmith had suddenly slipped away, promising to meet them at the palace.

"The Silversmith is a mysterious one," said Morbrecia. "She's my sister's best friend but even Charm will never understand her peculiar ways."

"I like her," said Sesame.

"So do I," said Morbrecia. "She has special powers and uses them wisely." She paused for a moment before adding mischievously: "Maybe the Silversmith could teach me a trick or two!"

The four girls floated on golden sunbeams and landed, light as feathers, on their feet. They were in the heart of a circular maze, and in the middle stood a pot of bright, red poppies. The Silversmith was there to greet them.

"Fairday, Charmseekers!" she said. "You're just in time for the party."

"Oh," said Hayley, feeling confused and excited at the same time. "Will someone *please* tell me what's going on?"

"Tell you later," said Maddy.

"Promise," said Gemma.

"Everything," said Liz.

They followed the Silversmith out of the maze, along narrow paths, round and round . . . until they came to the entrance and stepped into the palace gardens. A carriage had just drawn up, and out stepped Princess Morbrecia and Sesame. Maddy would have dashed through the flowerbeds to hug her, but the Silversmith gently held her back.

"All in good time," she whispered.

So they waited patiently, while Sesame knelt before Queen Charm (wobbling only slightly) and presented her with the bracelet.

"Sesame Brown!" exclaimed Charm, taking the bracelet and holding it up for everyone to see. "We meet at last. Your quest is over. You have shown great courage and faced many dangers to bring me my bracelet. You have saved Karisma! Thank you, Sesame. Well done!"

Just then the Silversmith stepped forward.

"Your Majesty," she said. "May I present Maddy, Gemma, Liz and Hayley. They're Charmseekers too and have all played a part in finding your charms."

Sesame was SO surprised to see her friends she let out a yell of delight. But there was so much cheering from the party guests that no one seemed to notice.

"Three cheers for the Charmseekers! Hip, hip, hooray!"

Then Charm turned to Morbrecia and the two sisters embraced.

"We're sisters," said Charm warmly. "From now on we must be friends too!"

"Yes," agreed Morbrecia. "We have *so* much to talk about!"

Dork was standing to attention nearby. Girls, eh, he thought. How they love to gossip!

❋ ❋ ❋

Sesame glanced at her watch. Before when she'd come to this magical world, her watch had switched to Karisma time. But not now; the display showed 18:50.

"Help!" cried Sesame. "*My* party starts in ten minutes. We must go."

"And so you shall," said the Silversmith. "I'll make sure you arrive in time. But first, Her Majesty wishes to give you these tokens of our appreciation."

For Maddy, Gemma, Liz and Hayley, the Silversmith had made friendship bands, and to each was attached a silver heart, inscribed with their initial. And for Sesame, her special Seeker, there was a bracelet, which *looked* just like Charm's magical bracelet – with thirteen silver charms!

The Charmseekers were thrilled and put them on at once. Then everyone joined in and sang The Song of Charms and cheered the girls again and again.

"Thirteen charms on a silver band,
United hold our world in hand.
May this gift for good Queen Charm,
Keep Karisma safe from harm.
One and all, beware the day
Charms and bracelet break away.
Together they must always stay!"

After many more goodbyes and fond farewells, it was time for the girls to leave. They were never quite sure how it happened, but suddenly they were flying through time and space in a golden haze of stars, until THUMP, BUMP, THUMP, BUMP, THUMP! – five girls landed in a giggling heap, back on Sesame's bed.

Jodie and Nic popped their heads round the door.

"It's seven o'clock," said Jodie.

"Everything's ready," said Nic.

And through Sesame's bedroom window came the beat of Crystal Chix. It was going to be a great birthday party!

Twelve

Much later that night, after everyone had gone home, Sesame sat in her room and talked to her teddy, Alfie.

"I've had the best day ever," she told him. "So much has happened, I can't believe it's all true."

She looked at the photographs of Silver, her very own pony, and of Kee-Kee the orangutan she would help to support, thanks to her grandmother Lossy. She'd had a fantastic disco and made lots of new friends – and soon she'd have a new mum too. Jodie and her dad were very happy together, and she loved them both.

And then there was Karisma! How would she begin to tell her family about that wonderful magical world and all the friends she'd made there? Her quest had meant so much to her and now it had come to an end.

"I *will* tell them," she said. "Tomorrow. I'll tell them everything in the morning." She stifled a yawn and stretched. "But tonight I'm much too tired!"

Sesame unfastened the charm bracelet – *her* charm bracelet – and put it in the jewellery box, where she would always keep it. Then she took off her necklace, and felt it warm and tingly to her touch. For one startling moment, Sesame thought something unusual might happen – and in a way it did. She opened her locket and looked fondly at the tiny pictures of her parents – Nic and Poppy. Then, as she looked at her mother, she thought she saw for the very first time a resemblance between the Silversmith and Poppy. It made her happy to think there was someone far away in another world like her mother . . .

Sesame closed her locket and placed it in the jewellery box, next to her bracelet. It was then she noticed the engraving on the back of her locket.

It was her initial 'S'.

Thirteen

The Silversmith sighs contentedly. Her Seeker's quest is over. The last magic candle has long since flickered and gone out. The precious charm bracelet has been returned to Queen Charm, and soon all will be well in Karisma.

The two moons of Karisma rise over Mount Fortuna and in the velvet night sky, the Silversmith looks at a bright star and thinks of Sesame. Perhaps across the vastness of time and space, her Seeker will see it too.

Acknowledgments

I owe a debt of gratitude to all those who have worked behind the scenes at Orion Children's Books and beyond to bring the *Charmseekers* books and their thirteen delightful charms to you. Since it would take more space than this edition allows to mention individuals by name, suffice it to say that I'm hugely grateful to my publishers and everyone involved with the publication of this series. In particular, my special thanks go to: my publisher, Fiona Kennedy, for her creative and skilful editing; my agent, Rosemary Sandberg; Jenny Glencross and Jane Hughes (Editorial); Alex Nicholas and Helen Speedy (Rights) Loulou Clark and Helen Ewing (Design); Clare Hennessy (Production); Jessica Killingley and Jo Dawson (Marketing); Pandora White (Orion Audio Books); Imogen Adams (Website designer – www.hammerinheels.com); Neil Pymer, the *real* Spinner Shindigs, for kind permission to use his name; and last, but by no means least, a million thanks go to my husband Tom for his inexhaustible patience, critical appraisal and support along the way.

Amy Tree

Join me, Sesame Brown, in the magical world of Karisma – and you can be a Charmseeker too!

For more about the books, regular Charmseeker updates, fun and games, and everything you ever wanted to know about Sesame Brown and her friends, visit

www.charmseekers.co.uk

Join the Charmseekers

at

www.Charmseekers.co.uk

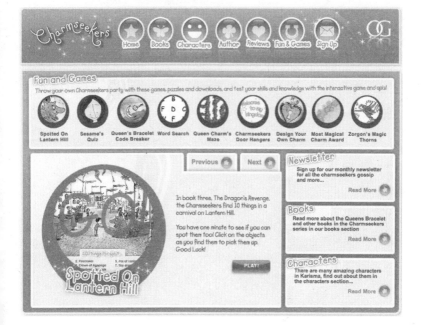